Her Royal Highness

THE ROYALS
BOOK FOUR

C. R. RILEY

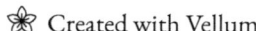

Hermosa Islas

This book is dedicated to all the moms out there raising amazing families. It is hard work and each one of you deserves an award. Keep doing what you're doing and enjoy each day because before you know it, those babies will be grown.

Note from the Author

Her Royal Highness mentions a stalker, which I understand may be a subject some of you would rather avoid. It doesn't focus on the stalker's acts or mention details, but a great deal of the book is tracking down this person. I wanted to warn anyone, just in case.

Reader Discretion is advised.

Prologue

ANGELA

13 years earlier

I'm not sure how we got here, but I cannot for the life of me seem to care.

I must admit I'm surprised to find the Captain of the King's Guard, Sir Edward Perez, standing at my door, soaked to the bone by the rain. It appears he's been out here for a while debating on whether he should or shouldn't be banging on it at this hour.

While he works for the Royal family, I am no longer considered his concern. My ex-husband made that clear the day I walked out of his office with the intent to leave him. He voiced it loudly to anyone listening. The only guard willing to stand up to him was Edward. He put himself between the King and myself when he was certain harm would come my way.

It wasn't a new reaction for him. He'd been placing himself between us for several years when life with the king got messy.

Made it his responsibility to ensure I stayed safe while he sat and talked with me. All while I did my best to cope with living a life full of lies.

This man and I had become friends, but only friends. Even though there may have been an attraction, one neither of us would dare act on or admit, friends were all we could ever be. His loyalty, after I walked away from that life, remained with the King. I've not seen or spoken to him without others present since that day. Our encounters were always focused on matters regarding the children, the heirs to the kingdom's precious *throne*.

I'm not sure what is going on or why seeing him standing there feels oddly familiar. And for the life of me, I cannot seem to care why that may be. It isn't as if I am doing anything wrong anchored in this spot admiring him. I am no longer a married woman. Haven't been for three years now. I can admire whoever I wish to without guilt.

This man is available, as far as I know. A single man, married to the job he does, opting to pass on ever having a wife and children. A few rumors are floating around as to why that may be, but one cannot always believe what others presume they know. No one can possibly know what we ourselves have never acted on or admitted. After I left the palace, nothing ever went anywhere, our friendship even seemed to fade. And had there been anything more, it seems logical to expect his intentions would be revealed before now. More logical for him to keep the lines of communication open at least, instead of remaining silent.

So why is he here? Why are we staring at each other, afraid that if we move or speak something will spark the desire energizing the air?

There can be only one explanation on why he made the trip and I begin to panic. "Is there an issue with the children?" I hold my breath while I wait for him to respond.

Sir Edward shakes his head fervently as his grip tightens on his wool trench coat. "I'm not here because of the children."

Relief washes over me as I take a step back and motion for him to enter. Once he is inside, I close the door and linger there for him to explain further.

"I probably shouldn't be here." Edward pauses and looks anywhere but at me. "In fact, I should go." Conflict overtakes him, making him appear unsure about his decision to show up unannounced to my home in Prieto. "This was a mistake. Have a nice evening, Angela."

Before Edward can open the door and escape with such a horrible explanation, I block it with my body. He drove all this way, stood in the rain for what looks like hours. Therefore, I plan on finding out why. "What was a mistake?"

He shivers, his soaked clothes visibly the source. Not even a man with his physique can fight the chill in his state of saturation. He may be strong and healthy, but he will not remain that way if he doesn't dry himself before bolting.

"You're cold and wet. At least dry off before leaving. We cannot have the Captain catching a cold." I lift my hands and place them on his shoulders to help remove his coat.

Edward immediately grips my wrists to halt my movement. It is then our eyes lock. For the first time since we've known each other, I allow myself to get caught up in them. His handsome green-hued eyes set my entire body on fire like never before. It's so overwhelming I almost don't hear his next comment.

"Fuck me."

As the phrase stumbles from his lips, I shiver, but not because I'm chilly. While I know he is not actually asking me to do just that—even understand his words are a slip of tongue that happens when you find yourself in a curious situation—it is as if my mind envisions the act and reacts. Realization washes over me on why we never once took the time to get caught staring or touching longer than those quick, brief moments.

I'm no saint, not by a long shot. King Ramon and I fell into bed months before we ever became engaged. I wasn't even a virgin when that happened, I lost mine before I set foot on Hermosa Islas soil at age sixteen. I understood my fate was to become the future queen to a country and man I knew nothing about. Before I promised my life and soul to such an existence, I decided I was going to allow myself to live a bit first.

I find myself speaking my next words as I grasp how long it's been since I've been allowed to really live. "Yes, please."

The shock in his eyes has me snickering like some silly schoolgirl. "Did you not mean that literally? Because that would be a shame since you drove all this way to do just that. I am certain I'd very much enjoy being fucked by a man like you." I'm not even sure how I mustered the boldness to speak, but I'm not sorry.

If the response in Edward's gaze reveals the truth, I'm almost positive I am about to get just that and possibly more. He blinks several times as the lines in his face harden. I'm not sure if he is surprised by what I expressed I would like him to do, or more to do with me doing something so unladylike with a man who just showed up in the manner he did.

It is out of character for me to jump so quickly into bed with a man. However, for some unknown reason whatever is transpiring between us advises me I should act. I know him better than I have any other man, trust him even. So, while I would not do this with just any chap, falling into whatever this is with Edward seems almost natural. Like fate.

"Are you okay?" I act braver than I feel when he simply stands there instead of responding.

Edward growls as he takes a slow step toward me, my wrists still in his hands. "Do not tease me. You have no idea how long

I've thought about you like that. If my King knew, he'd have taken my head a very long time ago."

"Which one?" I snicker, completely flabbergasted by the words leaving my mouth. My eyes travel to the large outline behind his trousers all on their own. I do not know what has come over me, but I revel in the feeling of being so bold and free.

He releases me to pace down the lengthy entrance of my home. Only to stop when he is thirty strides away and turns to face me again. There is no denying he is a man fighting with himself and his desires. "This is wrong. I shouldn't be here."

Almost four years have passed since I fled the palace with him by my side. He insisted on escorting me because he didn't believe I'd be safe until I was off the premises. It was him who drove me and my children to De la Pena Citadel, then made sure we were secured and protected before he headed back.

I've often wondered why when he left that day it felt like the end of our friendship. Sir Edward had been an ear I could count on when frustration set in. Sat with me the night I'd blown up and made a wreck of the dinner dishes. He always found a way to be there when my husband was screwing it all up, not once caring how his behavior affected me. It was comforting to believe I had one friend who offered me support and understood why I eventually walked away.

How had I not caught on to the reason why that might be, until now? Why had I been so blind to this man? How had I never seen what I am seeing now and not acted on it? I'd been so imprisoned in my inadequate life with a husband who never saw me, I had overlooked the one man who likely didn't want to see me but had anyway. Duty over desire had kept him from revealing his true self to me, protecting both of us until this moment.

When I begin to move, he speaks again. "He will not allow this to happen. Even now, he will discover a course to put a stop to this. My life could be in immense danger should I dare to do all those things I've dared to dream of doing. You deserve a man who can..."

Despite the fact he is a foot taller than me, double my size all the way around, I almost knock him off his feet when I practically jump him. It takes all his strength to keep himself steady until he can locate the closest wall and trap me against it. Tugging on his wet clothing, I strip him of them as fast as they will fall.

"You reminded me of an *anjo* the first time I saw you stroll into the garden," he whispers in my ear before he nips my neck. "A fallen beauty who stole my breath away."

His words barely make it through the fog that clouds my mind, but I remember that day as well. Ramon moved us into the palace two days prior to him taking the throne. Our boys were six and three. They needed to run off some energy and my husband was becoming impatient. I'd taken them to the garden to do just that, all while providing him the space he required to keep the peace.

An hour later Edward had been sent to retrieve us. What he came upon when he found us was me and my sons splashing around in one of the many fountains, laughing, enjoying life the way boys were meant to. He'd watched until I'd noticed him. I had blushed at how crazy we must have looked. I was soaked from head to toe, my cotton dress clinging to me. The boys were no better.

It was the expression on Edward's face that sent a warm intense fire down my spine. My husband never looked amused when he discovered me playing with his heirs. He always wanted them to be proper unadventurous children who snubbed all those beneath them. I, however, desired to teach them the joys life could bring, even if it meant I'd have to suffer a scolding and lecture for letting them act like little boys. Edward had regarded us as if he was really seeing me, and I hadn't been seen in almost ten years.

I grab his face and force him to look at me again now. "For that long?"

I swear the man blushes. "It was when I first took notice. I never allowed myself to give it much thought. You were my Queen, my King's wife. When he began embarrassing you by his actions, not appreciating what he had been blessed with, that is when I couldn't help thinking on how I would."

My lips find his again, and I whisper, "I am not his any longer, Eddie." I use a name I've heard a few of those closest to him use, wanting to make this more intimate.

A sadness washes over his face. "But my loyalty will forever remain with him, the realm, until his time ends. Which means I cannot really be with you because it would..."

"Then have this night with me. Show me what it could have been like had we been handed a different set of cards when we entered this world. Make me yours for a night and remember this night to get you through all the others. I know I will forever relive it for as long as I live."

He does just that. Not only for the night, but we spend the entire weekend together. We soak it all in and pretend no one will ever find out or be allowed to take this away from us. But when the day for him to depart comes, it turns out to be harder than either of us imagined. Tears are shed as a finality of what can never be settles in, making me wish for things that are beyond even my reach.

Edward is a man who places his loyalty above all else. A moment of weakness prompted him to my door. But it will not keep him there. Therefore, I'll be forced to deal with it. I vow to forge ahead the best I can. Promise to do what I need to do to get over the man who could have brought me happiness for longer than one weekend. I hate myself for not realizing how hard moving forward was going to be after experiencing something I will never get to have again. I chose the game we played and now I have to live with my choices.

CHAPTER 1
Edward

The Royals

Present Day

I've sat in this spot for the past three years and watched the CCTV similar to how a stalker might. No matter what I am doing, at seven-forty every morning, I make my way to the room where we go over surveillance tapes, and then I wait.

While waiting, I do what needs to be done. I often review surveillance videos my staff has flagged. Today I pull up last night's videos of Castile Vicente, the home of Her Royal Highness, Angela Iglesias. She moved there shortly after Prince Esteban and Princess Winfred purchased their family home. Until then, her residence was within these walls where I could keep better watch over her and Princess Gabriela. Meaning I didn't wonder what she was up to or who stopped by to visit. I only needed to check the log sheets. I could still do that I guess, but instead I choose to watch.

I keep an eye on the clock while I survey the front gate to her home. Stop it when a car pulls up around seven so I can get a closer inspection of the license plate. My blood boils when I recognize it instantly. I know it well. It's the same fucking car that has been showing up to her place frequently for several months. I fast forward and wait to see when it leaves, nearly coming unglued when the timestamp reads midnight and nothing. It isn't until fifteen minutes after two that the car finally departs, and I want to punch something. My mind is going completely haywire deliberating on why this person stayed so late, envisioning all the activities that went on behind closed doors.

My arm buzzes, alerting me of the time. Automatically my eyes find the correct screen as a black Escalade pulls up and is waved through. It continues to the side entrance where the guards are waiting to escort the King's Advisor to her office so she can start her day. I watch until she is inside, knowing very soon she will pass by these offices.

Like I have done every day since her return, I slip on my suit jacket, straighten my tie, and run my right hand through my hair. I gather my clipboard, pen, and my empty coffee mug. Then I step out the moment they are approaching so I can appreciate her with my own eyes and not through a camera's unclear pixels.

She presents the loveliest vision, as always. Dressed in her pantsuit, the navy blue one that hugs her curvy form. Today she opted for a sweater with a high neck, concealing it from my view. My mind starts to wonder if there is a reason for her choice in sweaters. Her long black hair hangs effortlessly down her back, exactly the way I believe it should be. She's not paying attention; it seems she's more interested in something on her phone.

I realize I shouldn't do what I am about to do. That this is childish and petty, and I'm a grown man who should act like one. But after what I discovered only moments earlier, accompanied by her unusual behavior of not watching where she is going, only encourages me.

I step out just as she walks by, causing her to run smack into me, sending her phone flying and then sliding across the marble palace floors. The scents of jasmine and honey hit me hard and nearly have me forgetting myself.

I reach out to steady her. "Good morning."

It is as if she doesn't even take notice of my solid frame, instead more concerned with the phone she was gawking at. Even starts to reach for it when one of the guards with her goes to hand it back.

But I am way quicker than her. Snag it first and then glance down, only to discover it locked. Not a problem for me. I unlock it with ease and am now the one staring, powerless to look away from the image displayed.

"Do you mind?" Angela reaches for it again, unable to retrieve it when I shove it in the inside pocket of my suit jacket.

I turn to the men escorting her and give my orders that will not be questioned. "Escort her to her office..."

"My phone, Sir Edward." Angela presents her hand as if expecting me to oblige her.

"Will be returned to you shortly. I require a cup of coffee first. And then it seems you and I need to discuss what is going on." My feet are moving to take me to the lounge just across from us. "I will allow you fifteen minutes to prepare yourself."

Her back straightens. I do not miss the stubborn nature she often displays when pushed. It alerts me I am going to need to cool my jets before I do something stupid. I know she would not appreciate it if I handle this how I'd like. Our relationship has a long way to go before I can ask her what she would prefer, me bending over the desk and fucking her until I felt better or me spanking her arse for not sharing with me she had a problem. I'm not a man who enjoys the latter, not really, but I might enjoy spanking and fucking her all at the same time.

I am fuming. At least now I see why she was unable to take her eyes off her screen. I nearly swallowed my tongue at the sight of her naked climbing out of the natural hot spring pool. Thankfully, it was the back of her and most of that was still immersed in the water. I only distinguish it as her because I recognized the tattoo so low on her back it usually stays hidden.

The picturesque queen bee with colorful jewels is only a few inches in diameter, but the details are amazing. There is a Spaniard semblance to it, making it known that she never planned to lose that piece of her. The crown surrounding the bee's head is full of jewels. There are beautiful dangling gems all around. It displays an ambiance of power and prestige that cannot be denied. I recall it all very clearly. Remember the story she told me about why she got it, while I did my best to memorize the art and then show homage to it.

"When did you get this?" I asked while kissing the tattoo slowly.

"A week before the wedding." Angela peeked over her shoulder at me with lazy, dreamy eyes. Light brown eyes that had rolled back in her head when she finally let go and given in to the pleasure I'd been determined to give her. *"It was my gift to myself. My fate had been sealed. And while I was at peace with my final decision, knew what I was agreeing to when I accepted the ring Ramon presented me, it didn't mean I had to conform completely. Or that I agreed to allow him to dictate what I could and couldn't do. So, I got that to make a few matters very clear. He hated it, and that was precisely the point."*

I do not doubt that King Ramon recognized what she was expressing. It was a fuck you to all that he thought he would take from her. It stated that Angela was still a strong Spaniard Lady, and would continue to be one. Placed there to remind him he would never take her heritage or break her spirit. It shouted that she was the queen bee, the one who would rule the hive she would be a part of. He may be King one day, but she would be Queen, and in a hive, the queen is the one who keeps the worker bees in line.

In my eyes, it was the sexiest fucking thing I had ever seen, yet a reminder of why she and I had to end our brief affair. Her ex-husband would not take kindly to me courting what was once his, a woman far above my status as a Royal Guard. I'd have been dismissed, humiliated, and blacklisted at the very least. And while the practice of executing a man for defiling a member of the royal family was long forgotten, I did not doubt my head would end up on a proverbial chopping block.

I need to get to the bottom of what is going on now. Figure out why someone would send her a photo like that. Gauging from her expression, as she headed down the hall, I'm concluding it was not one sent by someone she was familiar with, or if so, then it was not a welcome exchange. She appeared disturbed by it. And that bothers me. It also suggests that there may be more behind this than I know. I now must figure out exactly what, how long, and why.

It seems my plans for the day have changed. If my suspicions are correct, everything about my schedule has likely been altered.

I yank out her phone to look at it again. Begin flipping through this particular correspondence, an unknown number. Note that for some reason she's not reported that this is not the first time she's received such a message. After further investigation, it appears this has been going on for months. Granted not the same number, but the same M.O.

Now it is me who I am angry with. If I am correct, the reason she may not have mentioned these incidents has to do with me. The tension between us since that weekend so very long ago is strong. It often is mistaken as dislike for one another, when in reality it is our attraction. An undeniable chemical reaction that if not handled correctly could explode and take out all those we have fought to protect.

Her return to Aragon has intensified it, made it more dangerous. Put me extremely on edge. And with each passing day, each moment I do not act or attempt to clear the air, it only builds and gets worse. I felt her pushing, tempting me to interfere with her life, but so far, I've not taken the bait. While I've been willing to speak with her, work out the details surrounding her children, taken her words to heart. I've not dared to consider why she has come to me directly with her concerns. Why our exchanges seem to mean a great deal to her. Why when she leaves, it takes all that is inside of me to not go after her. All those years I trained myself to stay away. I realize now by doing that I've allowed someone else to get closer than they should have and put her in harm's way.

Now it is up to me to correct that. To decide if I am a man worthy of her, or a coward who is too afraid to do what he should have done the night he gave in to desire.

CHAPTER 2
Angela

The Royals

I 've been sitting here almost an hour impatiently waiting. I cannot believe he took my phone hostage. He had no right.

It's infuriating how my body melts whenever he is around. There are times I wish I'd sent him away that night when he came knocking. It would have been so much easier to never have known what I was missing than to know and be unable to have it.

I thought things might finally change after Ramon's untimely death. I didn't expect him to come immediately. I understood he had his hands full. Not only was he responsible for the investigation and all the inquiries about how something like that could have happened on his watch, he also held himself liable for not knowing all there was to know about Sofia and Ramon's relationship turmoils. It was impossible to keep up with a man as promiscuous and powerful as Ramon. His private affairs only continued to grow worse after I left, and that made him careless. Which had made Edward's job that much more challenging to keep him safe.

Edward's focus, in the beginning, I understood, would be

on keeping the next King safe. Fix all the holes he thought needed to be fixed to ensure what was done to Ramon never happened again. And I was thankful Antonio had a man with his experience to protect him, a man determined to not let another King die while he was in charge. But it had consumed him so much he'd forgotten I was waiting. So, I continued to live my life and tried not to become bitter with each passing year.

And when I thought our time had finally come, a night he stopped by my quarters in the palace after a long exhausting day, I'd been wrong. He'd shown up to fume about my son, who was not taking his security as seriously as Edward believed necessary. I'd sat in my living room and watched him pace the length a hundred times over, while he ranted about how many instances Antonio had broken protocol since Larkin entered the scene.

"I'll talk to him." I was finally able to say those four words when he took a breath.

"We employ these safety measures for a reason. He cannot just go off-script to chase tail." Edward plopped down into one of the chairs and looked exhausted.

I stood and walked over to the bar area, poured us each two fingers of bourbon, then strolled over and handed it to him. "He's in love, not heat. You of all people should be able to see that. When has my son chased tail?"

Edward swirled the liquid around in his glass as he studied it closely. "Touché."

I returned to my seat on the couch and couldn't help but wish he'd come for other reasons. Had he shown up for those reasons, I'd have gladly helped work out all the tension he held in his shoulders. Instead, we talked about how he should approach Antonio to make him see matters through Edward's eyes.

I'd walked him out hours later and began to understand no matter what we felt, we were never to be. There would forever be something standing between us. His loyalties laid with his job, and I was a distraction he could not afford.

That is the relationship we have found ourselves in these last four years. It was better than how the previous nine had been, when he barely acknowledged me. But it was also slightly more painful to be near him, knowing his programming to avoid was stronger than his desire to give in. Once seemed to be enough for him. I wasn't sure I liked what that insinuated; how different our time together must have felt for each of us.

It had also been the reason I kept quiet about being hassled by an unknown. The text messages were new, a much bolder way of contact than all the others. It seemed riskier, honestly, than the previous anonymous letters. Maybe not, though, since the number changed every few days. On the days I'd attempted to respond to a few, my messages quickly bounced back.

And while I understand I should have said something to my head of security, I knew doing so would mean he'd be required to report it to Edward. The very reason I had opted to ignore it and pray it went away on its own. One year and six months later proved me to be wrong. When Edward finds out how long I've been keeping this quiet, heads are going to roll. Mine, along with every person responsible for my protection.

The heat, however, should fall on my shoulders. I never once brought the seemingly normal, office-looking mail and packages that were delivered under false pretense to them. Nor had I dared to mention the flowers that were assumed to be sent by an admirer, yet held hidden messages tricky for most to decipher. The only reason I had was because whoever was determined to get under my skin granted me a key.

Today's message had done just that. Upset me enough I'd forgotten where I was and why it was so important not to give myself away. Now it looks like I will be required to sit down with him and explain. I had been provided ample time to come up with one hell of a story. A whole extra forty-five minutes and thirty-two seconds to fabricate a tale that was believable. But my mind has only been able to focus on the fact that someone has been watching me way closer than I'm comfortable with.

Meaning, I've made an error in judgment, not reporting it the moment I realized I had a complication. The problem being a stalker. This individual appears to be growing bolder to determine how I will handle him or her.

Yes, it could very easily be a her. This isn't my first. I've had several misguided devotees over the thirty-five years I've been a public figure, longer maybe. I didn't realize it back then, when I was only a teenager of sixteen, but there had been a person determined to interfere, hoping to make me look bad in Ramon's eyes. When it didn't work, this person backed off. It wasn't until later I came to understand that person had been my first lurker.

I need a drink to deal with everything weighing me down. I'm pouring myself a glass of red wine when my secretary, Rebecka, announces a visitor. I don't bother looking up at the one knock announcing their arrival. Instead, I stare at the stem of my wineglass and follow the last few bubbles popping as the wine airs.

When the door closes and then locks, I shiver. I'm not sure why he has locked it, but it seems he does not want someone to disturb us. As I pick up my glass, I glance up and am surprised to find someone besides Edward in my office.

How could I have forgotten that I had a meeting with Borras Rossi? He is an Italian, the CEO of a company my son has an interest in. Since Antonio is currently out of the country with his wife and children, it is my job to speak with him to see if we can help one another out.

Borras is a smooth, well put together man. A few nights ago, we had a nice dinner where he did his very best to persuade me we should be more than business acquaintances. I'd walked away wearing a smile, knowing I at least still had it, even if I passed on his offer. One thing I never did was get involved with married men, and this man was married.

I reach underneath the bar and push a small button to disengage the locks. There are several of those little buttons around this room intended to keep me safe while in a private meeting. Along with a handful more that set off silent alarms should I feel like I need security to enter unannounced.

"Drinking so early?" Borras chuckles as he strides toward me.

"It's been a crazy morning already." I reach for a highball glass, drop two ice cubes into it before I pour him a splash of scotch, and slide it his way.

"You remembered?" Borras seems pleased. "Should I take that as a sign of things to come?"

"No," I answer as I grab my glass and stroll over to my desk. "Take it as a gesture that I hate to drink alone. You are married, Mr. Rossi. I do not get involved with married men."

"If I were not married, then you'd consider it?" he replies in a confidant tone.

I am about to acknowledge him when the sound of my door slamming stops me. If there isn't damage to the frame, with the force it took to make such a racket, it would surprise me. Standing there, looking rather fierce, is Edward. And it seems he did not appreciate Borras' suggestion.

I take an exhausted breath and sit down. "Sir Edward, you are late. I am in the middle of a very important meeting with Mr. Rossi. You will need to return later when my schedule is free. You can check with Rebecka on your way out."

I'm not sure why I thought that would work. Perhaps because most people do not question me and follow directions when I give them.

Edward, however, isn't most people, which means he ignores me and addresses Borras instead. "This meeting is over. You need to go. Now."

I stand again rather abruptly. "That is not possible, Sir Edward. Mr. Rossi is on a limited schedule and we have business that needs to be addressed. It will only take us an hour." I glance over at my diary displayed on my screen. "It seems I can rearrange the rest of my day to accommodate you."

His rich green eyes bore through me, making my skin feel hot and uncomfortable. It has been way too long since I've had a gentleman caller. I may need to plan a trip soon so I can rectify that.

Edward turns, but instead of heading for the door, he makes a path to the bar. "I'll wait, then."

I roll my eyes at the arrogant man. "This is a private meeting. You will need to wait in the outer office."

"I'm sorry, Your Royal Highness, but that just isn't an option." Edward lifts the glass he poured and takes a sip. "It seems you are stuck with me by your side until further notice. No private meetings. No going anywhere unaccompanied. You and I are going to be spending a lot of time together."

My entire body shudders at the thought. Maybe a trip will not be necessary. This could be my chance to get this man to finally admit there is more between us than just a working relationship. But at the same time, I do not appreciate being told how I will spend my days. It is not his decision to make, it is mine. I am the one making those calls. He works for me and he seems to have forgotten that.

I pick up my phone. "Hello, Rebecka. I need you to get Travis, please."

Edward straightens and rolls his neck. One of his tells that displays he realizes I'm about to call his bluff. "Travis cannot help you."

A few seconds later my head of security steps inside looking rather amused. "You sent for me, Madam."

"It seems Sir Edward believes I am in need of tighter security. I want you to inform the team of this and take Sir Edward with you when you do. Once you two work out the details, please let me know." I tap my desk with my nails. "Does that sound reasonable to you?"

Travis glances over at his boss, who is currently pouting in a way that makes him look irritated. "I'm missing something here?"

Edward slams his drink down and heads for the door. "This is the last private meeting you get Angela, enjoy it. Moving forward, you and I will be attached at the hip." His green eyes find mine. The heat displayed proves his words were not only meant as a metaphor, but a very real threat that has moisture damping my knickers.

When the door closes, Borras leans back in his chair and studies me closely. It seems he's picked up on the tension between us.

"Now it sounds as if you believe your company deserves a tax break? Why exactly is that?" Time to move this meeting along so I can deal with Sir Edward my way. And like that, we are discussing business instead of why a man stormed into my office as though he had something to prove.

CHAPTER 3
Edward

The Royals

The moment Angela stood up to me, all the blood in my body headed straight to my cock. It wasn't the first time she'd given me orders, her previous position as my Queen had her ordering me around occasionally. While it was rare for her to do so back then, there were those times she would put her foot down and demand to be told the truth.

The very first one was right before I heard the dishes crashing in the palace galley. It had been her seventh anniversary to King Ramon. She had sent their two eldest children to have an evening with their grandparents. Lorenzo was only a few months old, so he was spending a few hours with his au pair, Helena. Angela had her husband's favorite dinner prepared to be served in their private quarters. My guess was so that afterward, the two could celebrate like married couples often did. When the king was two hours late, I was summoned to their residence.

"Is there a problem my Queen?" I asked after stepping inside only to notice she'd gone above and beyond to make it a special night.

My Queen was wearing a dress that any man would appreciate. I remember having to do my best not to consider inappropriate thoughts about the woman posed in front of me. It wasn't a simple task to do with her standing there like a wife ready to take down a husband I thought deserved her wrath.

"Where is he?" she demanded, knowing I knew but was sworn to secrecy. "You're here, so he must be as well."

My mouth went dry at the thought of breaking her heart on an important night like this. "He is." I had to be honest with her and was then forced to watch her maintain her composure, even though her chocolate-brown eyes appeared watery.

"Where? He's not here, where he promised to be. So where is my husband? Is he... is he entertaining?"

My gaze fell to the floor as I nodded once, hating every second of this.

"Take me to him," she demanded, using that voice that said she would not be denied.

"I'm not sure that is a wise idea, Madam." I tried discouraging her, but knew she would not be denied to witness it with her own two eyes.

"Is it an emergency?" I asked as we headed for the door. "A matter you can only discuss with him in person and not relay in a message through me?"

"It most certainly is." Angela hadn't even hesitated with her response.

"Then I should probably warn you..."

"Don't. Just take me to him and let Ramon warn me himself if he feels the need to do so." Her determination had me reminding myself who she was married to and why it was a terrible idea to allow my thoughts to run wild.

I did as she requested, knowing the King would have a few words with me later about it. Walked her down to one of the guest quarters in the west wing of the palace. When I went to knock, she stopped me, ordered me to use the key she knew I had in my possession. As soon as the lock disengaged, she stormed in and headed directly for the room the noises were emerging from.

She'd stood in the doorway, disgusted by what she found. Watched for way longer than I was comfortable with, and right before I was about to interfere, she spun on her heels and tore off. It appeared her presence had not been noticed, and that fueled her anger even more.

I allowed her to go while I remained behind to intercept my King if needed. Hold him back so she could retreat to their quarters to get all that rage out in private. I'd stuck around for twenty minutes, forced to listen to him and his young mistress get it on, never once aware we caught them red-handed.

Upon my return to the family's quarters was when I stumbled upon a crowd gathered just outside the galley. It took no time to realize why they were all standing around astounded by what was taking place inside. I'd sent them all on their way quickly before daring to take a step beyond the closed doors.

What I discovered had my feet planted firmly in place while I stared. Dishes were flying one by one across the large kitchen. Fine china that many would have considered irreplaceable, priceless heirlooms. To this woman, they were exactly what she needed to make herself feel better about a man who was openly betraying her. Since the birth of their third child, the King had entertained a number of women inside the palace walls. Her warnings fell on deaf ears and my guess is when he hears what she has done, he'll realize she's finished playing.

When the last dish went flying into the brick wall, my Queen heaved a heavy sigh before sinking to her knees. Her head tumbled into her hands and the sobs that followed broke me like none I'd ever heard before. I knew time was limited before someone would reenter the kitchen. I was not about to allow one of the staff to find her a disheveled mess like this. It was my job, after all, to protect every member of the Royal family, her included. The very reason I scooped her in my arms, allowed her head to drop to my shoulders and then carried her through a private passage that led us back to the King's quarters. When we arrived, I settled her gently on one couch, doing my best not to let the scent of her get to me. Then marched over to the bar and grabbed two shot glasses and a bottle of tequila.

I took my seat in the chair next to hers, set the bottle and shot glasses on the table between us, and topped them off. Shoving one glass closer to her, as I snagged the other and downed it swiftly. As soon as she had done the same and shook the cobwebs out of her head, I asked, "Did you eat anything earlier?"

Tapping the glass, she admitted, "No, but keep them coming, anyway. Who the fuck cares? Not me."

Her bluntness made me chuckle, pulling out my phone to order some food. I'd heard her swear a few times, and each time it sounded foreign. "I cannot be held responsible for giving my Queen alcohol poisoning. Therefore, I am ordering us some very good greasy food to help soak up as much of it as possible."

It has been years since I've thought about that night. It was the night Angela and I became more than acquaintances. The moment she and I formed a real friendship. We drank the entire bottle of tequila while devouring the greasy bar food I had brought in from my favorite pub. It was how I initiated her into my world of a second-class citizen and showed her just how we dealt with issues involving the heart.

King Ramon hadn't even bothered to return home that evening. I'd asked Helena to put Angela to bed when the time came. There was no way it would have been wise of me to place myself in that position. After I dragged my body back to my quarters in the guard residential area, then and only then did I dare to think about how close I had come to making the biggest fucking mistake of my life. Drinking with a beautiful woman, who hit all my high points, was not the smartest thing I've done. For this reason, I'd made sure moving forward to limit my intake to a bare minimum and restrict hers as well. No need to get us both in the sort of trouble we could not get out of.

Over the next few years, I found myself sitting with her while King Ramon made a fool of her repeatedly. I never understood why he refused to value the woman who remained by his side and supported him the best she could. But a woman can only be expected to take so much. The day he declined her calls when she went into early labor was the final nail in his coffin. It was also the day I fell flat on my face for the one woman I knew was completely out of my league and above my status. The exact moment I came face to face with the reality that my life would be complicated and unsatisfactory for a very, very long time.

King Ramon had sent me back to the palace to deal with his wife. I believe he did so because he recognized I cared for her—not understanding how much I cared, but knew I'd not let anything happen to her or the baby she was carrying. What he hadn't realized was that by doing so, he was also sealing his fate where she was concerned.

"Your Majesty," I beckoned when I entered the family quarters.

The youngest Reyes boy, Lorenzo, greeted me. He was holding a lacrosse stick in his hand, wearing only his underwear, a toothless smile spread across his adorable face. "Hi. Mother is lying down in her bedroom. Helena is with her."

"Where are your pants, Prince Lorenzo?" I could not help but grin about him taking full advantage of the situation.

"I took them off hours ago. I'm practicing and got too hot in the clothes I put on this morning. You want to see me score a goal with the sock ball Jorge made me in hopes I'd not break something while horsing around?" The young prince bounced the sock ball in his net like a pro.

"Maybe after I check to determine if your mother needs to be taken to the hospital. In the meantime, go put on some pants. We don't want the press getting another picture of a young prince

without his britches on." I ruffled his hair as he rolled his eyes, but ran off to do just that.

Now it was time to determine if my Queen needed the doctor called. I got the impression she did, but was in denial. The woman had an extremely stubborn streak that few understood how to handle. I had learned the best means to do so was sometimes to be equally as stubborn and pull the *it's my job* card when necessary to make her see reason.

The moment I entered the master suite, our eyes locked, and I knew we were way past the point of this being a false alarm. She was panting, sweating, and sitting in a pool of liquid that had a reddish tint to it.

"Helena, call Dr. Brooks and inform him it is time. We will not be taking her down to the infirmary this time. We will deliver this little one here and now." I gave the orders as I began slipping out of my suit jacket and removing my tie. "Have Jorge take the prince to the garden. He need not be around for this. Call down to the control center and instruct the guard to advise King Ramon to get his arse to the palace now."

Helena left to do just as I'd ordered, leaving me alone with my Queen. As I rolled up my sleeves, I took a seat on the bed and grabbed her hand. Tears were streaming down her face as she did her best to remain the strong woman she pretended to be. But in this moment, she was a mother, terrified that the child she carried may not live past that day. I was not about to let her encounter that day alone, even if my King was not man enough to be here. I would do whatever I needed to do to make sure she noticed someone cared.

It was the first and last time I witnessed someone give birth. I sat with her through the entire process. Wiped her brow, offered her my hand to squeeze, held her up while she pushed because the doctor was afraid she'd not have the strength to do so. It had been a day I cherished for reasons I didn't like to admit or think about.

The little baby girl was smaller than most, but not so small they worried for her health. That would come a few years later, another failure King Ramon would choose to make, causing even more issues for him.

What I remember most about that day is this. I remember thinking that if Angela were mine, I'd never have let her go through that alone. Recall what it felt like to hold her, encourage her, and then watch her give birth to the most beautiful little girl I have ever laid eyes on. I will never forget the expression on her face as she held her child in her arms, relief to have it over and done with, knowing her child would be okay. And the sadness in her eyes as another reality washed over her: the fact she knew her marriage was no more. I walked out the door to give her back her privacy. Certain I was not likely to ever experience something so lovely because the woman I had fallen in love with could never be mine.

CHAPTER 4
Angela

The Royals

My meeting with Borras lasted longer than first predicted. I expected Edward to be pacing the corridor when I escorted the man out. The only person there, however, was my secretary, who was busy at work and never looked up when he left.

I considered making my way down to Edward's office, but in the end, let him come to me. While I waited, there were plenty of tasks that required my attention.

A half-hour passed before Rebecka announced I had a few visitors and a special delivery. I'd been expecting the first, but not the second. It worried me with all that had been going on today already.

Travis entered carrying the massive bouquet so large I wasn't sure where to put it so it wouldn't be in the way. I settled for the table between the couches on the other side of my office. Motioned for both men to take a seat while I located the card to determine who I had to thank.

Edward studied the arrangement carefully from his post with a sour expression. It was clear he believed I was receiving them from an admirer, but I had my doubts about that. The card proved I'd been correct. Funny how a lovely arrangement can suddenly become anything but. My love for flowers had me studying the meaning of them for years. I always found it interesting when someone sent yellow carnations to a loved one, not realizing they mean rejection.

Today's arrangement to the unknowing eye would mean nothing. A beautiful mixture of deep purple iris and goldenrod. Not something that would be sent every day, but still very lovely. Given my royal ties it might even seem appropriate knowing the iris often represents royalty. But when you add in the goldenrod, it holds a completely different implication. The flower warns the receiver to be cautious, and after this morning's text, the significance does not slip past my radar. The card has three words printed in block letters and makes the hairs on the back of my neck stand. *My Royal Highness.*

I shove it into my pant pocket before I take a seat opposite Travis and Edward. Crossing my ankles, I then wait for one of them to start this meeting I have no desire to be part of. When neither utters a word, I encourage them to do so. "Did you two come up with a plan?"

Edward speaks, but it has nothing to do with why we are here. "Who are the flowers from?"

I'm not sure why I suffer the need to poke the man, but it seems I do. That can be the only explanation for my answer. "An admirer who thought it would be nice to let me know they were thinking of me."

I recognize that was not the correct way of handling this situation with all that's going on right now. What I said after all is not a lie; they obviously wanted me to appreciate they were thinking about me. However, it would have been best to come clean and disclose that the person who sent me the text likely sent me these. It was meant as a warning to let me appreciate they are standing by and advising me to be cautious about moving forward.

And because these men have a job to do, that job being to protect me from these types of threats, it would have been wise to hand all evidence over to them. Allow them to weed out the important ones from the not so important. But because I've been dealing with this for the last eighteen months on my own, it seems old habits are hard to break.

"What did the card say?" he continues, making the vein in his forehead pulse slightly. "Are they from him?"

For the first time in a long time, I am truly confused by his words. "Him?"

"Yes. Him. Is he thanking you for a lovely evening? I assume you had a lovely evening since he didn't leave until after two this morning?" Edward grumbles while he crosses his arms like a jealous, sulking man.

"Are you fucking kidding me?" I spit out. "You think Ivan sent these to me?"

He ignores me as he resumes his ranting. "Are you fucking him? Is that why over the last couple of months he has been returning to your home a few times a week? I thought more of you than that."

I cannot believe Edward is having a man strop in front of Travis like this. It is completely embarrassing for more than one reason. First, what I do on my time once I am home is my own damn business and nobody else's. Not his. Not those even responsible for my security. I may entertain who I wish when I wish to do so. So fuck him. Who does he think he is bringing this shit up in mixed company? If he has a concern that he deems needs addressed, then he can ask me about it when we are alone. He should not openly be discussing this in front of Travis, the man in charge of my security and nothing else.

I realize Travis is extremely uncomfortable at the moment,

which only adds fuel to my own fire. "Travis, could you excuse us for a moment?" I am fuming, ready to wring Edward's neck.

Travis bolts to his feet quickly and is out of my office before the arsehole I am giving the death stare to can correct his mistake. Not that he seems aware he has made a dreadful mistake by acting foolishly.

"Who the hell do you think you are? Let me make a few matters perfectly clear to you, Sir Edward." I use his title so he knows I mean business. "What I do in my personal time is none of your concern, not today, not tomorrow, not ever if I don't want it to be. So fuck you and your pompous arse."

"So that is a yes," Edward growls, rising to his feet. "Fucking Ivan Batista is the man you have chosen after all these years."

I've heard about all I can from this man who has done nothing to express there is something between us. "I will fuck who I fuck. You have not been around offering your services. You're too much of a fucking pussy to admit that I'm who you want. Which means you don't get to voice your opinion on matters surrounding my personal life." I'm not sure I have said that word so many times in one sentence before, but when it comes to this arsehat, my filter disappears.

His pacing halts and he stands there with his back to me. Those broad shoulders moving with each breath he takes. When his head shifts slightly, the pain reflected in his eyes has me giving him what he wants to know.

I relax in my seat, fold my hands in my lap, then tell him the truth. "I'm not fucking Ivan Batista. He's not coming to my home to visit me."

"Don't lie to me." His voice hitches and it becomes clear his thoughts are eating him alive.

"I have no reason to lie to you, Edward. Ivan comes to call upon Clara." I smile thinking about what I witnessed the other night. "They have been seeing one another for a few months now.

I gave them my permission to carry on in the manner any normal couple might since she lives in my home. I have no idea what happens once they retire to her separate living quarters. Not my business to know. Sounds like maybe they have finally taken matters to a new level though. Good for them."

He slowly whirls around. "Your chef? Isn't he a little old for her?"

I can feel my face scrunch up, annoyed. "I don't see how that is my concern, either. She's a grown woman. In her late forties. Plus, they seem extremely happy together."

Edward nods and takes another inspection of the bouquet. The wheels inside his head are spinning fast.

"The flowers are not from him. I'm not sure who they are from, honestly. Probably the same person who finds fun in sending me a photo of myself inside a space where I was meant to feel safe. Funny how that goes away when you are violated like that." I pinch the bridge of my nose and stand. "Would you like a drink?"

"No," he grumbles.

"No? It might take the edge off," I advise him as I make my way to the bar. "You look as if you could use a drink, Eddie."

"What I need is..." He stops once he is blocking me from going any further. "What I need is this."

I don't have time to protest, not that I would have. It has been so long since I've had the pleasure of his lips on mine. They are like coming home after a long draining trip that zapped all my energy. Just like the first time when he kissed me. The night he showed up out of nowhere and ruined me for all others.

"God, you feel amazing." His large arms wrap around me to tug me closer.

I will admit it is easy to collapse into him again. Something about this man seems to make me act before my brain can think too hard. The taste of him, as his tongue slips past my lips and finds mine, is intoxicating. I have to grab onto his shoulders so I remain steady.

When he draws back, I want to voice my disapproval. It would be so easy to demand he allow me the right to experience all of him again. It is evident by the hardness pressed into my belly he's ready and willing to do just that. I crave for him to make the first move this time, though. I need it to be his decision, not mine.

His forehead drops to mine, and he stares into my eyes. I can see the pain behind them. The war he is fighting again, and fuck me if it doesn't hurt. My hands urge him away. I cannot be a part of what we did before. This time it will have to be all or nothing. It is the only way I'll survive.

"You should go," I enlighten him. "Let Travis and his team handle this. It will be better this way."

Edward's eyes squint as he studies me. "If you think I am going to let Travis deal with what is mine to handle, then you have lost your fucking mind."

"I don't wish to put you out, Edward. The last thing I want is to get in the way of all you've worked so hard to keep separate." It is time to stop this and move on so both of us can have a life.

As I reach for the doorhandle to invite Travis back inside, Edward's hand lands on mine. The heat that transpires between us steals my breath. In one swift action, he has me spun around and pressed against the door, reminding me of that first time again. I'm overwhelmed and fall apart before I can stop it. It has been a long day and I don't have the energy to figure out his motives.

"Hey." I hear his voice next to my ear. "Why are you crying?"

"I'm tired. So tired of everything. It's exhausting to have to put on a face for everyone, including you. To pretend that when you walked away that day it didn't slice me to my core."

Large arms scoop me up and carry me across the room to the sofa. He settles down on one and just holds me, cradles me like no one has ever done before. I've not been taken care of in so long, not really. Ramon and I were married for eighteen years. The first four were the best years we had, and they were nothing to brag about. I didn't marry him because I was madly in love. I married him because I had a contractual obligation to do so. And once I ended up pregnant, it seemed the proper thing to do for the next heir to the kingdom. But love was never a part of my marriage or my relationship with Ramon.

After him, I'd had a few lovers, not many but a few, to help me get past the pain he caused. During our marriage, I had been faithful completely to him, devoted to my duty as his wife and the country's queen. So when it ended, I needed to do a few things for me. I wanted to feel alive again, engage in activities that made me feel like a woman. The night Edward came calling is when I learned what I'd missed out on by choosing that life.

Sure, I got four amazing children for my time, and for that reason, I would not dare change any of it. But my title cost me even after I'd walked away. It had kept me from a man I believe could maybe love me if he weren't so devoted to his duty. And that made me hate all those things about this life I was forever trapped in; making me tired and miserable in my own skin.

"I'm sorry," he tells me as he gets comfortable. "I'll do better. I promise."

I want to believe him, really, I do. But until he can prove he will do better, I am not about to let myself fall for him again. Not if I am able to help it. But the way my body is relaxing against his, I'm not so sure I will be able to stop the inevitable.

CHAPTER 5
Edward

The Royals

A few days have passed since Angela melted down in her office. We sat there in silence for what felt like an eternity. Eventually, we got around to discussing her problem, and why not informing her team put everyone in danger. I did my best not to yell or scold her for hiding it for so long, especially after I learned just how long that had been. I'd even been able to convince her to hand everything over to Travis so his team could play catchup.

Last night, I met with his team and learned so much more about how serious her situation was. This is why I'm not in my usual spot in front of the CCTV monitors waiting for her to arrive this morning. Instead, I am in her office, seated at her desk, with all the offending evidence spread out before me.

I am doing everything I can to maintain my cool, but the longer I study the letters, printed out texted messages, and photos, the more difficult that becomes. I will admit the first few lines of communication seem harmless, but that isn't her call to make. Once you add in all the others, going back an entire year, it is easy to identify a pattern. A scary pattern that conveys things are about to escalate rather quickly now. And that scares the fucking shit out of me.

I've been sitting here most of the night. My suit jacket is long forgotten. My tie was yanked off hours ago and tossed to the side. I shed my waistcoat early this morning when it felt too tight on my skin. The sleeves of my shirt have been rolled up for hours now, and the top three buttons on my shirt are undone, making it easier for me to breathe. When I checked my reflection in the mirror an hour ago, the thickness of my five o'clock shadow had almost doubled. My once auburn beard is showing signs of age, it is whiter than I remember. I'm convinced the last few hours have added at least a hundred more highlights.

I hear her approaching, speaking to Fernando about what she believes her schedule will be. I have news for her, I've rearranged it and cut out those events I deemed unnecessary. Until I have this all figured out, Her Royal Highness will go nowhere without me.

"Oh." Angela stops at the doorway and appears surprised to find me here. "Is there..."

"Fernando, please leave us. I need to discuss a few private matters with Her Royal Highness." I stand and then wait as she takes in my untidy appearance. "Once I'm done, we will head back to Castile Vicente and settle in for the long haul."

"I have a particularly heavy..."

"Not any longer." I stroll over to the bar and reach underneath for a mug. "Coffee?"

I hear the door close and then the distinct click of her heels moving across the marble floor. The moment she steps onto the carpeted area I know. I push the mug toward her and then set out the creamer she likes. Once my own cup is filled and ready, I take a sip and finally glance up at her. She has moved over to her desk and is frozen in place while she takes in all the items covering every inch of it.

"You lied to me." I don't dare move from this spot; afraid I'll do something I know she is not ready for. "I dislike being lied to, *Anjo*."

Using the nickname I graced her with on the weekend we spent together way too long ago catches her attention. Over the last few days, I've done nothing but think about our time together and her. I realize how foolish it was letting her go without a fight. The way my avoidance was about me being afraid to get close to another person, to let someone in again, more than it was about her ex. I have my own hang-ups only a few people know about. In order for this woman to be able to understand, I'll need to share that with her one day soon. Which makes me feel ill and shaky, because I don't enjoy talking about my private life and the failures behind it. But I'm willing to do so now, because I refuse to permit one more day to pass without her understanding who I am and what I want.

"I didn't mean to lie." Her weak voice warns me she is on the verge of losing it again. "I just hated to admit the truth."

Angela reaches for one of the many items on her desk, picks it up, reads it, then sets it back down while juddering her head. I catch her swipe at her cheeks a few times and then I watch as her entire body quivers. She is staring at it intensely, and I do my best to figure out why that may be.

"Can I ask you something?" Angela speaks so softly I barely hear her.

I make my way over and stand next to her, letting all the awareness of what is us takeover. It's been like this since we gave in and let desire control us. Before then, being in the same room was tolerable. Now it takes everything inside of me not to touch her, not to want her. I've never felt like this before, never had this kind of connection that could physically be detected when one stood this close without actually touching. Another reason I avoided her after we came together. I knew it would be impossible to hide.

"What is it you'd like to ask me?" I lean forward and stare at a photo, it's one of her during her first year as King Antonio's Advisor. I'm not sure how I know this, but I do.

"When you've figured out who is behind this, will that be the end?"

My head jerks in her direction, so I have time to study her face. Why would she ask such a foolish question?

"You are a man who does his job and does it well. Put all you have into the work you have devoted your life to. So, what I'm asking is, am I also part of the job, or am I more?"

I spin until my hip lands on her desk and I can rest my arse there. "You have never once been a job, *Anjo*. How do you not know this?"

It's true. Even before when she was my Queen, it felt like more than part of my duty. My life's devotion was to protect her and her family. After our time together, it only emphasized that. And when King Ramon died on my watch, my allegiance to this family took on a whole new meaning. I was and still am determined to keep them all safe for as long as I am alive.

She reaches for something hidden deep in the pile of pictures and tugs on it. Once it is free, she holds it while she explains. "I never thought much about you and I like that until the day you came to me. Before then, you were always just Sir Edward, one of my husband's most trusted men. A friend eventually, after that dreadful night when I went a little nuts and broke some china. I'm not sure how I never saw it or felt it, but I didn't. Why do you suppose that is?"

I run my hand down my face as I give her my honest answer. "I don't know that there was more to it than that back then. It wouldn't have been wise for us to get together like that considering the circumstances. It wasn't so wise to do so when we did."

Sensible or not, I have never once regretted our time together. I've regretted my response to it, but not the act of getting my chance to love her. If given the chance to go back, I would still make the drive and spend the weekend with her. What I would change is the way we progressed, my reaction to my fears, because I now understand how those have erected a barrier between us that should not be there. And since that isn't possible, then I'm going to figure out how to remove it and get us on the right track.

She hands me the photo she's been studying, and now I'm the one staring at it mesmerized. "It may not have been so obvious to us, but it was to someone else."

"Fucking hell, when was this taken?" I flip it over but cannot place it, there of course is no date on the back.

It's a photo of her holding a very young Gabriela, two at the most. I'm in the background looking directly at them. I had no idea anyone was taking this photo or even paying attention to me. Probably the reason my guard slipped, and I allowed my face to give away every thought passing through my mind.

I glance up and am nearly taken back by the sadness written all over her face. "That was taken the day before I walked into Ramon's office and told him I wanted a divorce. So tell me Eddie, when this is done and I'm no longer in danger, will you once again be the man in the background or will you step into the light?"

I toss the photo onto her desk and reach for her hand. Seeing her this way cuts me like nothing else. It's time to let her in on a secret I have, one that changed me so many years ago when I was a young man. "Did you know I was once married?"

The stunned expression on her face says she did not. It's no surprise. It was before I was assigned to the King's Guards. When I was still going through the training required.

"I met my wife when I was sixteen. We were so young and stupid." A small smile spreads across my face. "Married by the time I turned eighteen, she was only seventeen, but she lied and said she was older."

"Just babies." Angela is really looking at me now.

40

"We didn't think so. We thought we were adults ready to live a long happy life." I let out a huff and shake my head. "Damn, we had no fucking clue. But we were in love, and that was all that mattered to us. Flora was an amazing woman."

Angela quickly picks up on my use of the word was and flinches. "What do you mean was? Oh, Eddie." She steps closer and places her hand on my face. "My sweet man, what happened?"

Tears fill my eyes like they do each time I think back to the day when my world was turned upside down. "There was a fire at the factory where she worked. Five people died that day, Flora was one of them. Two days before, we found out we were expecting our first child. I was twenty and had been on cloud nine, bragging to all the recruits that I was going to be a papa. But instead, I became a widower who decided nothing was worth that kind of heartache."

Angela rakes her fingers through my hair. Sadness written all over her face. It's clear she's assuming I'm telling her why we will never work, why I cannot have a relationship. "I understand. Of course, I understand."

My arms wrap around her and haul her body as close to mine as possible. "I was wrong. Heartache is part of living, and something we experience no matter how hard we try to avoid it. Losing Flora the way I did was devastating. My future was altered, and I was bitter for a long time about that. Devoted my life to the job and those I was sworn to protect, because I thought that would be the safer route. It wasn't.

"I never meant to fall in love again, never expected anyone could ever get past the walls I constructed. The funny thing about walls, sometimes while you are constructing them you pull others inside with you, those you feel also need protection. You believe you are doing so because it's your duty, when the real reason has nothing to do with that at all. A heart often knows more about what it needs than the mind wants to admit. It typically finds a way to overrule and leads the way."

Soft hands caress my face, trace over the worry lines embedded in my forehead, and then down until they circle my lips. "What are you saying exactly?"

My hands trail up her back. One finds its way into her dark black hair and forces her closer so that we are only a breath away from our lips touching. "I'm saying my job may be to take this son of a bitch down, and I will do just that. But if you are okay with it, I'd like to be more than just Sir Edward. I want to be the man you never knew you needed, the one who shows you how much better life is when you spend it with someone you love. Let me love you, *Anjo*, please."

Her lips find mine and I feel as if I've died and gone to heaven. I never meant to share so much with her. My intent was to speak with her about my plans to be her personal guard until this all was resolved. I'll admit I like this so much better.

CHAPTER 6
Angela

The Royals

We were forced to gather ourselves rather quickly after Edward's confession. Seems I have a few visitors who are very excited to see me. I'm equally excited to see them, I must admit, they've been gone for a month and I've missed them.

Once Edward has the evidence boxed, he carries it over to the door and places it on the floor. Then strolls back to me, tucks his finger under my chin, forcing me to gaze up at him. "I meant what I said."

Placing a hand on his arm, I do my best to let him understand I believe him. "I know. Seems we may have to make up for lost time soon."

A smirk forms on his handsome face. "How soon?"

"I don't know. I suppose when the need arises, I'll let you be the one who helps me take care of it." I'm not sure where I find the nerve to tease him, but I do.

His green eyes grow darker and a growling noise escapes from his throat. "Fuck *Anjo*, torturing me like that will only get you into trouble."

Rising to my toes, I kiss his lips and then share a little secret I know is going to drive him crazy. "Torturing you would have been informing you why I am in no real hurry, since I took care of things last night, alone."

I squeal when he yanks me against him, rubs his now hard dick into my stomach. "Fucking tease. I'll have you know your toys are going to feel neglected soon. Fuck *Anjo*, how am I supposed to walk out of here without everyone staring at my crotch."

"Sucks to be a man, doesn't it?" I laugh as I take a step back. "My grandchildren are waiting, Sir Edward. We will have to discuss all that later."

Again, he growls while he does a little adjusting before he picks up the box. Placing it in front of him to hide the sizable definition, he nods at the door. Right before I open it, he leans in and kisses my lips hard enough to make my cheeks flush and my heart flutter.

As the door opens, I am still dazed when I come face to face with my son, King Antonio. "Is everything okay?"

"Everything is fine. Sir Edward was just gathering up the paperwork we needed to go over so he can take it with him." I do my best to regain my composure and smile at two beaming faces. "Did you all have a nice trip to Japan?"

Both little ones are wiggling in his arms to get down. As soon as he sets his oldest child's feet on the ground, she comes for me.

"I'll be four soon," Nicolette reminds me. "Only five more days."

I envelop her in my arms and squeeze. "I know. I've got a present for you at my house."

"Just one?" She grimaces and Edward chuckles as he makes his escape.

I smile at her honest expression of disappointment. "One very large one and possibly a few little ones to go with it."

She nods in approval and then runs to the corner where she knows I keep a few toys. I love having my grandchildren visit me. I never want them to think this is a stuffy, boring office where children are not welcome.

As I stand, I stretch my arms to snag my grandson, Lucas. He is nearly a year old and a butterball like his father was at this age. If it weren't for his blonde hair, which he inherited from his mother, he'd be the spitting image of Antonio. After I've gotten a proper hug and slobbery kisses, he decides he wants down to go play with his sister.

"So, how was Japan?" I ask again, making my way over to the corner where I grab a seat in one of the chairs. "What did Larkin decide?"

"She was thrilled they asked her to join the team but said the time away from home and her family would be too much. Promised to be a second opinion if they needed one but has decided to not take on such a large project." Antonio sounds relieved and I cannot say I blame him. If his wife had taken on this project, it would have required half her time to be spent in Japan. I know he hated the thought of his family being separated, but I am proud of him for allowing her to make the final decision.

"What does that mean for her and Manchester International? The company is about finished here, correct?" I realize this is another big decision hanging over their heads.

"Three months and our contract with them ends." He smiles and I recognize the admiration he carries for his wife. "They have offered her a satellite office to manage here. She and Hope will run it. Those two are going to stay busy restoring all the historical buildings we have in Hermosa Islas. Eventually, they may branch out, but for now, the plan is to pick up new contracts and grow into the top historical architectural firm here."

"That's wonderful. I take it Dane has finally come to his senses where Hope is concerned then," I inquire about one of his guards and see him nod.

"Now why don't you tell me why Sir Edward was really here in your office." Antonio wears an expression that says he expects an answer.

I want to laugh at him for trying such an action on me. He may be the King, a powerful man who often gets his way in all things, but he is now and will forever be my son first. Giving me that look doesn't have the same effect it has on others.

"Mother."

"Antonio, don't. You might be my King, my boss even, but you are not about to intimidate me. I wiped your arse as an infant. Chased you around this very palace when you didn't want a bath. Forced you to sit in a room with your brothers until you all stopped acting out. So do not think you can give me the same look I have given you and make me spill matters that do not concern you." I stand and walk over to the bar to pour us both a drink. "It will not get you very far, my dear boy."

He softens slightly, knowing he has met his match with me. "What is going on that has put Sir Edward on edge?"

I also know that not telling him is not an option. If I don't share, someone else will, and then I'll have to deal with another man throwing his weight around demanding a solution. One is about all I can handle at the moment.

"I seem to have picked up a stalker." I pass him a tumbler and take a sip of mine before I look at him directly. "Nothing more than a few letters and photos. It's harmless. Someone wanting to ruffle a few feathers."

It's a lie, one I don't feel bad telling. I know my son well enough to recognize he'll go ballistic. Then he will not allow Edward or my team do the job they understand how to do better than anyone else.

Antonio swishes the liquid around as his mind spins. I know

he doesn't believe me; it's written all over his face. Thankfully we are interrupted by Alejandro and Beatriz when they come looking for him and the children. My son and his family have been gone a month, which means Antonio has so much to catch up on.

Alejandro is his personal secretary who is only doing his job, and Beatriz is the au pair for my grandchildren. After I've said a proper goodbye to my grandchildren, I am left with Antonio and Alejandro.

"You were saying." Antonio starts to get comfortable.

Alejandro however has business that require my son's attention. "I hate to cut this short, Your Majesty, but we have issues that cannot wait. Unless this is important, we really do need to start."

I could kiss the man. "It's not. Sir Edward and Travis have it all under control. You have a country to run. Go, so you can get back to your wife and children at a decent hour. When do you head back to Homero?"

Antonio downs the remainder of his drink and hands the glass back to me. "In a few days. She has business here first, and I'm doing my best to meet with everyone who thinks it's a must. Please listen to Sir Edward and follow his orders precisely. He's very good at what he does." My son kisses me on the cheek before he leaves.

I feel slightly guilty not letting him know how serious it all is. It wouldn't be the first time I've kept information from him. I wonder what Sir Edward will say when he also learns about the real reason Gabriela and I moved back to Aragon. It is buried in the report somewhere. Zane, another of my guards, and Fernando refused to leave it out completely. They did however agree not to mention it unless it seemed there was more to the story. At the time it appeared there was not.

I have to wonder if maybe this has been going on even longer, especially after I uncovered that photograph. My focus had been on Gabriela and Ramon, so I hadn't noticed Edward in the background before. I thought the message being conveyed had more to do with what happened the following day, a day I haven't reflected on in forever.

"I don't know what you want from me." Ramon stood there with his arms crossed, looking every bit the dominant male he was. "I've given you everything your heart could desire."

I stared at the photo hanging above the fireplace in his office. It would seem he has granted me a great deal, yes. Four beautiful children that I love beyond words. "Do you honestly believe that? Do you not think my heart might have possibly longed for more?"

"You knew what you were accepting when you entered this marriage. I never hid who I was from you. I told you early on what to expect, what a life with me would bring you."

He certainly did that. He never once lied about enjoying the company of other women. Was honest about doing so both before and after he convinced me I was the woman destined to share his life with him. I was a naïve girl who believed I could change him, make him fall in love with me after bearing his children. Be the one who could keep his eyes from wandering if I kept him satisfied in the bedroom. Our bedroom shenanigans had not been the problem. If one could hold a marriage together because of what went on behind closed doors, then ours should have been indissoluble. Ramon was an incredible lover, knew how to draw me out of my initial shyness, and then taught me all I needed to know. Seemed to enjoy doing it even until he didn't. Until he claimed he missed the variety, along with the mystery of the unknown.

I'd tolerated it as long as he kept his affairs quiet. I hated it, but I had allowed it because it was no surprise that one day he would likely take a mistress or two. He had made that very clear before we took our vows. Although, each time it happened, each time someone regarded me with knowing eyes, it broke me. It shattered me completely when he chose one of them over his family. That was where I had drawn the line when I decided this was not the life that I had agreed to.

"It was not this, though. You have changed. You are not the man you promised me you would be." An argument he'd heard from me before, one he never stood there and took without a rebuttal.

"Nor are you the same woman. People change, Angela. I will hold you to the vows we made, the one where you promised to remain by my side at all times. To be my Queen who supports her husband, the King, until death." He wasn't about to back down; I could see it in his eyes.

"Well, times have also changed. I will not be embarrassed by you any longer, Ramon. I'm done. I'm taking my children and leaving. I want a divorce."

Until that very moment, I'd never been afraid of my husband. I was however terrified of him then. He'd never looked so unnerved and ready to show me he was in charge. "No!"

"It wasn't a question." I stood my ground, hoping that would encourage him to back down. *"I am telling you this out of respect for what we once had, but I am not asking you for permission."*

I didn't even see it coming until it was too late to prepare myself. The pain that shot across my cheek knocked me back a few steps. "I said no, and because I am your husband and the King, my word is final."

Shocked by his outburst, I decided the best thing for me to do was to leave. I'd told him what I had come to say, and now it was time to act. As I began to make my way for the door, his words slowed my departure.

"I'm warning you, Angela, you do not want to push me on this."

I yanked the door open before I spun to face him, "Your message has been received loud and clear. Goodbye Ramon."

When I stepped through the door, I immediately collided into a human brick wall. One that gripped my face gently and tilted it upward. A loud string of explicit words mumbled past his lips before a direct order was given. "Have a car brought to the back guard entrance to collect the Queen."

Ramon must have followed me out because he had a few instructions of his own. "You will no longer address Angela as Queen. She has decided she isn't interested in being your Queen after today. From this moment on, you are to refer to her as Her Royal Highness, a title she only acquires because of the children she has born. I want all her belongings moved immediately to De la Pena Citadel, along with Prince Lorenzo's and Princess Gabriela's. Everyone else stays put, training is still required, and it seems I'm taking that over."

Sir Edward nodded firmly as he tucked me under his arm and began escorting me away. It was an act often regarded as unacceptable, but Edward didn't always follow protocol when it came to me. Our friendship often overruled all else.

"Sir Edward," Ramon called after him, in that tone that made it clear he was not having it today. "Don't forget who you work for and where your sworn loyalty lies. It would be a shame for a man in your position to throw his career away for a woman who has become an enemy of the King."

I remember cringing at his suggestion where so many could hear. To make it seem as if his guard, who he often sent to help smooth me over, was about to defy his king in the worst of ways.

Edward paused and cleared his throat before he addressed Ramon. "I believe I swore to protect and serve all those in the Royal Family, not just the King. Protect them against all threats, even if that should mean standing between one of those members or the King himself. Did you strike her?"

"Are you questioning my integrity?" Ramon was pissed about being called out in front of those watching.

"Does your integrity need questioning? Her Royal Highness did not have that red welt on her face when she walked into your office. How did she get it?" Edward never displayed fear when *forced to take a stand, no matter who it was he was standing against.*

"Are you accusing me of something?" Ramon took a step toward us, and Edward did what he had always done, he remained firm. "Are you?"

"I am asking how your wife got that mark on her face."

Ramon said nothing, he too stood his ground while glaring at both of us. If he did not want to answer, that was his right. He understood nothing could be done unless I spoke out against him.

"How did you get the mark on your face, Your Royal Highness?" Edward asked while staring King Ramon down.

"It doesn't matter, it won't happen again." I gave him my answer, not wanting to make this situation worse than it already was. "Please, can we just leave?"

Ramon smirked before he spun around and strutted back into his office, knowing nothing more would come of it.

"Fucking arsehole is lucky I didn't witness him put that mark on your face." I'd never seen Edward so angry before.

"Sir Edward, please, leave it."

He took me under his arm and guided me down the hall to where the car was waiting. "Fucking hell, tell me this is not a common..."

"It's not," I told him, gently twisting out of his hold so he'd let me go.

I'm not sure he believed me, but he never asked about it again. When I got in the car Lorenzo and Gabriela were waiting inside with Helena. They looked a bit confused about why we were making a swift, unexpected departure. It shocked me when Edward joined us, sat next to me keeping a very close eye. When Gabriela unbuckled and then climbed into the empty seat beside him, he didn't even flinch. I knew it wasn't safe, but the sight of him settling her as she rested her head on his lap, the gentle pats he gave her, brought tears to my eyes. As soon as she fell asleep, he scooped her up and secured her back in the safety seat across from him.

"Thank you," I whispered.

"Always my pleasure. She's a special one. I feel a connection to her and hope that remains, even after." He reached over and took hold of my hand that was between us, gave it a gentle squeeze.

Lorenzo had been quiet until then. "Where are we going, Mother?"

My words were stuck in my throat, so Edward spoke for me. "To De la Pena Citadel, you three are going to live there. How exciting will that be?"

My youngest son's eyes light up. He loved the country home in Prieto. "Seriously? Like forever. No more of the stuffy palace where I am not allowed to run like I do when we are there?"

I nodded and smiled at him the best I could. "No more stuffy palace."

He did a fist pump into the air and started telling us all the things he was going to do as soon as we arrived. Edward sat there quietly holding my hand, offering me the comfort he believed I needed, and I never forgot how that felt.

CHAPTER 7

Edward

The Royals

It's been a little over a week since I was made aware of Angela's secret. I've barely slept. My days and nights have been crammed, going over every piece of evidence she handed over to us. Travis and I have analyzed the fucking shit out of every photo since she brought the other one to my attention. I shared more than I ever thought I would with him. As the man in charge of her team, he needs to know everything. Plus, I required his assistance. I wanted eyes that were unbiased and could analyze the evidence with the same assessment.

The good thing, if there is one, is that whoever this individual is, he/she seems to follow a pattern. If this pattern continues, then we have time before this person strikes again. At least a few days to prepare, so we can intervene and then figure out a way to track this person. Which is why I'd felt comfortable waiting before inserting myself and taking over completely. It wasn't her team's fault they'd missed the threat. This landed solely on Angela's shoulders. She'd allowed it to continue for way too long, and now they were playing catch-up, trying to locate the needle in one big fucking pile of hay.

I'm sitting in my office when my desk phone rings. "Captain Edward speaking."

"Three days in one week that you've missed my arrival and departure. You're slipping, or maybe I'm no longer..."

"Fuck," I growl, not realizing so much time had passed. "Don't go there. I'm sorry."

"Are you working late again tonight?" Angela's question throws me.

"I work late every night, *Anjo*. It's part of the job and a habit I've developed over the years. Why?" I flip through a stack of papers that require my signature when a small tap on my door catches my attention. "Hold on." I set the phone down and stand so I can answer it.

Standing there, looking amazing, is the woman who has been on my mind. She slides her phone into her purse, wearing a sensual smile. I've not seen her for a few days; our schedules have prevented it.

"I thought you left?" I take all of her in like a breath of fresh air. "What are you doing here?"

She studies her nails for a second. Her next words shock the fucking hell out of me and have me almost coming in my pants. "I believe I told you I'd let you know when I felt needy so you could help me take care of it. But if you are busy, I suppose my vibrator will do the job. It is one of the higher end brands and more than adequate at bringing me some release. I'll let you get back to whatever it was you were doing."

Angela only gets a few steps from me before she finds herself pressed up against the adjacent wall. Fuck if I'm going to let her walk away after that little speech. My lips attack hers until she melts against me. I'd forgotten what that felt like and suddenly cannot wait to get inside of her again.

"That is a good way to get fucked right here and now," I warn as I pull away to catch my breath.

She is flushed and panting, exactly how I love her. "Here in the hallway for all to see?"

My mind clears almost immediately and I jump back, having forgotten where we were. "Fuck, I'm sorry. That was inappropriate."

I cannot believe I pounced on her without warning. I've not lost control like that in years. I suspect the last time was with her. She seems to have that effect on me. During our affair we acted like sex maniacs and fucked about in every room we found ourselves in. It was as if I just couldn't get enough of her. I thought it was because I realized our time was limited and was doing my very best to get as much of her as I could. Making certain the woman never forgot me or how amazing we were together. I knew I'd never forget her; she was an unforgettable goddess who placed a spell on me and ruined me for all others.

A wicked grin spreads across her face. "Does that mean you will join me then?"

Stalking her, I snarl like an animal might when he is about to display his desire to prove himself. "I am going to fuck you in a way I have not fucked you in years."

Angela visibly shudders as she seduces me with her words. "I look forward to seeing if you can live up to your promises. My last few lovers never came close to the bar set by a certain male. He was, if I recall correctly, in a league all his own." At her last words, her gaze drops, and fuck me if my cock doesn't twitch.

I lean forward to kiss her hard when Zane interrupts us before I can do it correctly. "Captain, I hate to interrupt, but you insisted on being alerted should there be an issue."

We both compose ourselves and turn to where he is standing, studying the ceiling instead of us. There will be no masking the fact that Angela and I are about to make matters very complicated. I'm guessing Travis has enlightened his team that we have a past, one he only recently became aware of. It would make sense to do so. I'd have done the same, it was why I shared. And because Angela and I have not discussed how open we want to be, keeping this new blooming relationship from them is not only impossible but careless.

"Go on," I instruct him as I reach for her hand and head for my office.

Zane's eyes land on our hands, but he maintains his composure. "One of the guards posted at the main gate of Castile Vicente would like to speak with you. He says a package was delivered by an unknown sender."

I release Angela's hand as I retrieve my cell to phone the guardhouse. "Captain Edward, speak."

"We have a package here you might be interested in looking at," the guard on duty informs me.

"What kind of package?" I don't like this, not one little bit.

"A small rectangular box, about the size you might send a modest arrangement in. No window for viewing, though. There is a note attached, but no inscription on the outside. A delivery service dropped it off about fifteen minutes ago."

"And?"

"He had us sign for it. Nothing else. I questioned if he knew more, and he said he was just the delivery guy, didn't even know who sent the package besides what was in his manifest. His manifest listed the source as unknown."

"Bloody hell. Who allows an unknown package to be sent these days? I swear this world is full of idiots. I'll be there in ten." I hang up and try to decide how I want to handle this. I could allow her to come with me while I have a look at it, but my gut says to keep her far away for now.

"What's going on?" Angela squeezes my hand that she grabs again.

"How are Prince Esteban and Princess Winifred doing? I bet they would welcome a little company, an extra hand at the moment." I overheard her speaking a few days ago that the youngest is not sleeping well, keeping them up, even making their other child more irritable. It would be a wonderful distraction for her while I do my job, ease my mind a bit knowing she will be safe.

"Are you trying to get rid of me? Please tell me what is going on. Don't keep me in the dark." She tugs her hand free and straightens her back, looking like the powerful woman she is. "I have every right to know."

"Is that so?" I'm not sure why I feel the need to start this argument right now. "You mean like I had the right to know about this person now sending you threatening messages. How long did you keep that secret, Angela? A few hours? A few months? Oh wait, no! You kept it for eighteen fucking months and would have kept it longer had I not sent your phone flying. So, don't fucking tell me you have the right to know what is going on. If you'd have been honest from the very beginning, then none of this shit would be worrying me, turning my hair white before its time."

Zane thankfully retreated as soon as he realized we were about to have it out. I'm sure he knew it would likely lead to personal matters, and to keep things professional, he provided us some privacy.

"Fuck you." Angela spins and goes to storm out only to whirl back around with her finger aimed right at me. "Don't bother sticking around once you've checked things out. I'm no longer in need of your services. I'll stick with what has been working for these last few years. My vibrator will do the job just fine. At least I'll not be required to deal with an arrogant arsehole or his ego. I can enjoy a good long fucking without it making demands or promises it cannot live up to. I'll take that over a man any day of the week, sometimes multiple times without having to wait for it to get up again. No need to get your boxers in an uncomfortable twist. If I require an orgasm later, I'll take care of it all on my own."

By the time I've recovered from Angela's outburst and scramble after her, I receive a text reporting her team is leaving and taking her to her son's home. It's probably better this way so I can gather my control before doing something I'll regret. I am still in disbelief she dismissed me like that. Unsure how I want to deal with her, or all she felt the need to reveal. No one has ever dared talk to me like that, no one.

Fucking vibrator. Is she kidding me? There will be no more fucking vibrator once I get my hands on it. I'll tear the useless invention in half and then remind her why having an arrogant arsehole of a man is a thousand times more satisfying. Or better yet, I'll take that damn thing and use it on her while I do my best to demonstrate the reason I am better than a toy that can only do one fucking thing at a time. I may not be a young man anymore, but I'm not fucking dead. There are plenty of ways to keep her occupied while I recover between orgasms. I can do pleasurable wicked acts that her little rubber vibrating toy cannot.

While I'm driving, I grip the steering wheel tighter, wondering if Angela meant what she said. Why she thought she needed to dismiss me instead of talking it out like adults. The woman I know fancies a good argument. I'd witnessed her taking her ex down a notch or two more than once. So the fact she just stormed out bothers me more than it probably should.

I hit the button that will ring her, then swear in my head. If she ignores my call...

"What? I seriously cannot believe you right now. Whatever. I just talked to Esteban and the baby won't stop crying. He is at his wit's end. Danilo is being a typical three-year-old and not at all cooperating. Since you do not want me around while you perform your job, I decided it might be best to see if I can be of assistance." Angela doesn't even give me a chance to ask a question, meaning she likely expected my call. "I'll stay put until you grant my team the all clear. By the time I make it home, I expect you to be gone. I'm not feeling up to company tonight."

I am not allowed to counter because she hangs up, so the moment I pull into the lot, I grab my phone to text her.

> ME: Don't be like that.

ANGELA: Then don't keep me out of the loop. I know what I did was wrong, but if you cannot get over that, then this will not work.

> ME: Fair enough. I'll do my best to keep you informed, but you have to do the same. No more secrets.

ANGELA: I can agree to that. No more secrets moving forward.

> ME: Do I get to stay now or am I not allowed to do my best to make up with you? I think I would be rather excellent at making up.

ANGELA: We shall see. I'm not sure yet.

She's not sure yet? I take that as permission to stay and grovel. It has been years since I've groveled while I flipped the tables, making my woman wonder why she was mad at me in the first place. Years since I've wanted to do it even, which makes me consider how I walked away from this woman so easily that first time.

When I climb out of my car, I am greeted immediately by the guard on duty. "Sir Edward."

"Where is it?" I don't waste time with conversation, I never do.

I'm led to a room in the back. The package in question is resting on the table. Two of our investigators are giving it a once over. I quickly learn they have already x-rayed it for explosives. Thankfully, none were found. Our dogs have cleared it of any detectable substances. Which means there is only one thing left to do, open the box so we can take a peek inside.

This time when I call, I do so using video. I want her to see it with her eyes so she can tell me if she's received anything similar before. I asked the other men to leave before I called Angela, I don't need everyone to hear parts of this conversation.

"What is it now? You missed me?" She holds the phone out and I spot the little one in her arms.

"She's stopped crying?"

"It happens when someone not so frazzled takes over for a bit." She kisses the small head and I cannot help but long for what I have never had.

I don't have time to think on that now, though. "Have you ever received a package from this guy before?"

"No. And you don't know that it is a man, it could just as easily be a woman."

She isn't wrong. I've come across a number of female stalkers. Women can be just as dangerous as men. One's sex does not make a stalker any less of a danger. It all depends on the reason the stalking started. An obsession with the individual they are pursuing is common. Sometimes it is brought on by jealousy or someone the person they are stalking has once been involved with. Other times it can be an admiration gone bad, where the lurker suddenly feels wronged for some reason, and is now trying to correct the wrong. It is hard to know what can trigger a person to begin an unhealthy infatuation, but the longer it continues the more dangerous it becomes. One or both can be a situation that will end badly.

I cannot ponder on that right now or I'll lose my cool again. I switch the camera view to allow her to see what I'm looking at instead of me. I need to focus so we can put this behind us and get on with our evening plans.

"Hmm." I hear her make a noise I know means she's noticed something familiar.

"What is it?" I ask, holding the phone steady while inspecting the package so I miss nothing.

"It's probably nothing," she starts slowly. "And to be clear, if this is from the same individual who sent the other items, it doesn't necessarily mean the other similar packages were."

"What others? I thought you said..."

"Would you let me finish? I said *if* this one is from the same individual. You asked me if I have received a package from this person before, not if I have received any packages. I receive packages like this one all the time."

Maintaining my temper, I ask, "You've received something similar to this before?"

"Yes. Every couple of months, if that. Usually, it's delivered to the palace though. Rebecka always assumed I had an admirer who worked in the palace or possibly a frequent visitor. She would make a production of it when delivering the parcel and then force me to open it in front of her."

I switch the camera back so I can see her face when I ask her my next question. "Did you think the same?"

Her eyes divert away from the camera as if embarrassed about her answer. "I wasn't sure. It seemed logical, but then again it didn't. It also seemed dodgy, not something anyone working at the palace would consider. Most understand how it all works, how you take security seriously. That your team is thorough and should they catch wind that a person didn't follow the rules, heads could roll."

"So why am I now just hearing of this then?" I swear if my grip on the phone tightens any more, it will bust into a thousand pieces.

Taking a seat in what looks like a rocking chair, Angela adjusts the baby as she begins rocking. The phone then gets propped up against something so she is no longer required to hold it. Once she is settled again, I watch her face do that thing she does when she has something to say but doesn't want to say it.

"Why, Angela?" I push her because I'll be damned if I'm letting this go.

Her voice is firm but soft, to not disturb the little one she is cradling. "Because I knew you'd act a fool. Don't think that I didn't notice the way you would become moody when a male visitor stopped by, one you assumed had intentions."

"Because so many are like Borras and make assumptions about you, they should not," I grumble.

"And I've always handled them just fine. I never mix business with my personal life. You never gave me the chance to respond to Borras. Instead, you tried to throw your weight around and scare him off." She is getting irritated and if I'm not careful, I'll be back in the doghouse again.

"He wanted to fuck you, Angela," I growl.

"And just because that is what he wanted, does not mean it is what he was going to get. I've told many men no all on my own. I've been doing it for years, in fact. I don't need you to intervene on my behalf, I'm more than capable of turning them down on my own. And I believe you too wish to fuck me, making you not all that different from him. Now can we focus and move on?"

I want to protest her last statement because while she is not wrong, fucking her is not all I want. "For the moment, yes. Tell me, what was in the other packages you received."

"Open the box, Eddie, let us have a peek inside to establish if we might get a better understanding." She ignores my request and begins giving orders of her own.

Only because I'm just as curious, I am about to do just that, but not before I address her use of my less formal name. "So, I'm Eddie again now, not Edward."

"Edward is the man who often acts foolish. You can quickly become him again if you start acting out," she warns, but I notice the smile hidden just under those perfect lips.

I place my phone on the table allowing me to open the box while I tell her like I see it. "If Edward is the guy who gets to fuck you later, then I will gladly be him. Is he that man, *Anjo*?"

"No. I believe I've already explained this. I do not fuck arseholes. I have no need to." Damn if she isn't making me hard smarting off like that.

"So, it looks like Eddie is going to get his chance to prove his worth to you later tonight. I am looking forward to it." I take a chance to throw that in, getting her ready for what I hope will transpire between us when this is done.

"Open the box and stop. I'm not having this conversation with you." She rolls her eyes.

I open the package and stare at the contents inside. A gardenia and two rhododendrons tied together using a yellow ribbon, resting on a bed of torn photographs.

My blood goes cold right before it starts to boil when I recognize something personal. I never once thought I'd be staring at this woman after all these years. I'm not sure what it means, but when I get my hands on this person, they will give me all the answers.

"What's going on?" She leans forward and motions for me to move the camera so she can see.

"Did you once know someone named Florence? This would

have been years ago," I ask staring at the only other woman who had me tied in knots.

"Maybe, what's going on Eddie? You promised to not keep things from me."

I place the lid back on the box and pick up the phone. "Finish what you are doing and then return home. Do not go anywhere else. Do not tell anyone anything. Finish your visit and come to me. Do you understand?"

"Yes. Are you going to tell me what was in the box?"

I stare at the package and feel sick. "I will when you get here. I promise."

CHAPTER 8
Angela

The Royals

It was a few hours before I could leave and head home. My grandson was soaking up his parents' attention being back on him instead of his sister. I was more than happy to offer them a break, made a plan to stop by more often in fact. Winifred has been trying to do it all on her own and it is wearing on her. I remember what it was like to deal with little ones. Even with assistance it can be difficult.

I was not given a choice on using an au pair, the first night Antonio was home she took over on Ramon's orders. I'd only been authorized to nurse him throughout the day and once during the night. He made it clear we were not to be bothered like other parents. Our job was to provide the heirs but not necessarily raise them. It was a battle he lost eventually because there was no way in hell I was letting someone else raise my children. I'd seen the results that kind of practice produced. I wanted my children to be better. It took me a few long-drawn-out battles to get him to back off. There were customs he insisted the oldest two needed adhere to. I was, however, allowed to raise our younger children differently after the divorce. He was not about to take on more with them when he was too busy fucking his way through the kingdom.

Watching my son, Esteban, and his wife tonight brought me great joy. My son is the most amazing father. He took care of his son's needs and still pampered his wife who was exhausted. Ran her a bath while I entertained the children, then came and sat with Danilo and played blocks with him. They built towers only to knock them over like Godzilla, making the toddler laugh and growl like a little boy should. Liliana and I sat observing them while we shared a cuddle. The little girl was trying to decide what she thought of it all, unclear if she wanted to join them or stay safe in my arms. Winifred joined us again, looking so much better, just in time to feed her famished daughter. It was obvious my visit had helped, and I was happy to have been allowed to do so.

It wasn't until the drive back that I finally had time to really think about what Edward had asked me. Did I once know someone named Florence? It wasn't a common name. I hadn't heard the name for years.

I was only sixteen and had been in Hermosa Islas for almost four months. I hated it here. Hated all my classmates. No one talked to me. I was ready to return to Spain and forget about this country that seemed to hate me as much as I hated them.

I was studying in the library alone, until a girl I'd seen a few times pulled out the chair across from me and sat down. She dragged out her history book, the same one I was currently studying, and then waited. I glanced up to find her smiling.

"Angela, right? Duchess Angela is how I am to address you." She stretched out her hand. *"Lady Florence Castillo, but please for fuck's sake do not call me that. Call me Flora."*

I immediately liked her and her sassy mouth. "Nice to meet you, Flora. You can just call me Angela."

"Are you ready to tuck tail and run yet?" She laughed when I seemed taken back by her question. "I mean no disrespect. I'm just

saying if I were in your position, and all these fucking snobs treated me like I had the plague, I'd get the hell out of here too. Tell that arsehole of a Prince to find another sucker to rule this ungracious bunch of twat waffles."

The laugh that escaped me was loud and had everyone in the library turning to stare at us. "Forgive me if I'm wrong, but aren't you a part of this ungracious bunch?"

Her eyes lowered as she agitated her head in disgust. "Not for long. I'm making a break for it very soon. My boyfriend and I are going to get married as soon as he finishes his training. While I think he is crazy wanting to guard a prick like the Prince, it's been a dream of his for as long as he can remember. So who the fuck am I to stand in his way. As long as he takes me far away from all these high-nosed very tight arsed..."

I'd cut her off to finish while laughing, "... twat waffles."

She smiled so big her eyes shone in delight. "Precisely. If it walks like a twat and talks like a twat, then it's most certainly one big fucking twat waffle. This place is full of them and it is so sad to see a friendly person like you get pulled into this corrupt group without the proper preparation. You are so fucking lucky I refuse to let them eat you up and spit you out without the knowledge of how to handle them."

"How do you handle an ungracious group like this, Flora?" I inclined closer when she leaned in.

"First and foremost, you look them in the eye, and you don't look away first. Never ever look away first. As soon as they blink or flinch, you say this and only this." She bent in even closer and very confidently said, "Fuck you and the horse you rode in on. Now be gone before I expose that secret you believe no one knows about."

"What secret am I exposing?" I wasn't sure I could curse like that. It's not something my parents had allowed.

"Hell, if I know, but each one of these prestigious fools has one, and they will never ask you to tell them what it is. No fucking way

will they dare admit they are anything but perfect. But they will back the fuck down because if you really do know one it could ruin them." She reclined back and motioned at me. "So, let me hear you say that."

Another girl had snuck up on us while we'd been talking. "Oh, isn't this cute, the reject table."

I stood up, so that I was on equal ground, and stared into her cold black eyes. I did so until she got uncomfortable and looked away.

"You are so weird," she mumbled trying to make me feel she'd won. "You will never fair well with our dear Prince."

I took a step toward her confidently, forcing her to look at me. "Fuck you and the horse you rode in on. You may go now, leave me and my friend. Should you choose to not do as I have requested, I'll be forced to tell your friends how you've been sucking off their boyfriends behind their backs. That was you, right? Behind the science hall, on her knees pleasuring Lord Shelton?"

The girl spun around on her heels quickly and stomped off with her head held high. She had not been expecting that, and I'd proved I was not one to mess with.

Flora was gaping at me with amusement in her eyes.

"What? Did I do it wrong?" I'd asked when I took my seat knowing I'd not.

"Fucking hell, Angela. This flock of buzzards has no idea what they are up against. You are going to be one kick arse, Queen. I'm going to love watching them eat the humble pie you will one day serve them."

Florence and I had remained friends until the end of the year. She left for break and never returned. I received a letter from her a few months later informing me she had run off with her dearest Eddie and was living the best life. I'd forgotten about her once my life got complicated, but I'd never stopped thinking about the lessons she'd taught me.

I walk inside my home and hand my belongings to my maid as I ask her where Sir Edward is. She informs me he is in my office before she leaves, which is exactly where I find him pacing.

It is as if he can sense me watching him, because he stops and glances over at me. There is a deep pain reflected in his eyes, one that has my feet moving quickly. As soon as I am in front of him, his arms pull me close and he holds on tight.

I soak in his warmth as I do my best to bring him some comfort. "Lady Florence Castillo. I knew her for maybe a year when I was sixteen, we went to boarding school together."

His sigh is heavy as if he had already figured it out. "She hated that place."

"She did. Flora was one of the only friends I had while they forced me to attend the school the Royal Family had chosen to educate me on all things, Hermosa Islas. I was to learn etiquettes from the offspring of the elite who attended one of the best schools the kingdom offered. Although it wasn't good enough for the Royal Family's children, they were always sent abroad to further their education." I go on to explain how I met Flora and how she helped me uncover the confidence I would need one day. When I was through, I inquired, "Now why did you ask me about her?"

Edward releases me and begins his pacing again. I had almost forgotten how he loves to pace while he thinks. When something is bothering him, he paces. It's a wonder there isn't a worn spot in my ornamental rug.

My eyes glance around the room and land on the rectangular box he called about earlier. It is on my desk, open. I don't ask permission to look, this is my home and what is in that box was sent to me. I have every right to see what someone thought was worth sending.

A white gardenia and two red rhododendrons tied together with a yellow ribbon. The flowers seem like an odd pair.

Gardenias are often meant to resemble hope, beauty, and trust. Sometimes they can signify a renewal of a relationship or be used to encourage one to put your trust in something. I've also heard that if you see one in your dreams it is meant to make the message of the dream stronger.

All very significant when put together with what I believe the rhododendrons are saying loud and clear. In nature, these flowers can be poisonous. In my mind it only seems natural they were meant as a warning. They often are sent to warn the recipient to beware that danger is nearby.

These flowers are telling me very clearly someone is watching, has been watching. That this person knows who I trust, where my hope lies, and who my dreams have been about. Aware that we are about to renew a relationship we lost years ago. This individual is warning me to not go there or he/she will be forced to make all my secrets known. The ones this person believes will take me down. Ruin me along with the family I hold dear.

The message, however, only causes my blood to boil. It encourages me to prove my place now and forever will be where it has been for thirty-eight years. I will not bow to idle threats or let a person too weak to stand in front of me face to face intimidate me like this.

And then I notice the torn photos, used as a bed for the flowers. I don't bother to be careful; I remove the offending flowers and begin sorting through the tattered prints. They represent the life I've lived in this kingdom. My early years when I was still in boarding school. Flora is in a few of those, standing next to me while we attended an event. There are others as well, a few who tolerated me after she and I made friends. A collage of photographs representing those who have held some meaning in my life. Friends maybe, but it is difficult to have a genuine friend in my position.

The person who appears the most is now standing beside me.

Early encounters seem more professional, but as the years pass, it becomes unmistakable that we moved into something more. Even during those years when we barely spoke, when seen together there is an aura between us that speaks to a person watching closely.

"We have to be more careful." Edward picks up one of the torn photos and then tosses it to the side. "This person has been watching you for years. They are obsessed and they are getting brash. So, we need to…"

I grab his shirt and hold tight. "You are not dismissing me, Edward."

A wicked smirk takes over his face. "No, I am not. You are going to be sick of me before this is over."

My grip tightens as I tug him closer. "Not possible." My lips land on his.

I am tired of always being the one waiting for him to act. The first time I allowed him to walk away, let him be the one to make the call. I'm not doing that this time. This time I'm making the calls, taking charge, and making a few demands of my own. He cannot dismiss me or push me away. I'm done expecting him to pull his head out of his arse and do what should have been done years ago.

Edward seems dazed when I finish kissing him as if he isn't sure what just happened. Grabbing his hand firmly I spin and drag him behind me. I am pleased he doesn't put up a huge fight. That he follows my lead and shuffles his feet behind mine as I lead him through my home and straight to my bedroom suite.

"*Anjo.*" He tugs on my arm before we walk inside. "Are you sure?"

I lean against the door and tell him the truth as I see it. "It's either you or the vibrator. I do believe you wanted to prove why you were the better choice."

CHAPTER 9
Edward

The Royals

Fucking hell, it is about damn time. I've waited years to have another chance with this woman. The first time we were together it was so rushed and frantic I didn't get to enjoy it like I should have. This first time, however, I am determined to take it slow and soak in every moment as if it could be our last.

When we step into her bedroom, Angela releases my hand, so I close and lock the door. I'm not sure why really, no one is in the house with us. She lives here alone and has for a few years now. Princess Gabriela is away at the moment. She finished university a few years back. Now, she is doing some soul searching, hoping to figure out where her place in this world and family is. While doing that, she is taking a few classes to further her education and exploring some other avenues.

The only people left in the house are staff. They never leave their quarters unless summoned, never venture beyond the common areas of her home. Her team would only do so if an alarm went off, alerting them she was in danger. The only other time they check the home is when she is away, when they do regular inspections of the locks and alarms to make sure they are functioning properly. Meaning no one would walk in on us, but my instinct has me locking the door as a safety precaution, anyway.

"Fuck me, *Anjo*," I blurt out when I spin back around to discover she has stripped of her clothing and is standing before me buck naked.

"I'm jumping in the shower to wash the day off," she tells me before taking off for the bathroom.

I notice something I know was not there the last time I had the pleasure of admiring this woman's body. It was hard to get an impressive look at it because she moved so fast. But I'm not about to let that stop me. A shower sounds nice, it's been a few days since I had one. I'm tossing my clothes to the side as I make my way to her. I'll worry about picking them up later. Right now, I need to have a proper inspection of her left hip.

As soon as I step into the bathroom, the steam hits me hard. The sound of the water running and her humming brings back a few memories. I recall how she likes to sing in the shower, and by sing, I mean sing. The woman has a voice of an angelic cherub. Her songs are often in her native Spanish tongue and those she once enjoyed as a young girl. I stand in the open stall and regard her while I listen.

My eyes follow the water cascading down her dark black hair that covers her back. It follows the curtain of silk until it lands on the bumblebee tattoo I once worshiped. It's had a touchup since that time. Very bright and vibrant with color.

I drop to my knees on the hard tile and hear her squeal when I grip her hips and kiss the spot. My cock hardens fully while I pay homage to the work of art she placed there to remind her to stay true to herself.

"What are you doing in here?" She sounds surprised. "There is another shower, you know?"

I lick the tattoo and then let my tongue dip into the crack of her arse. The shiver that travels through her body encourages me to remind her how much she enjoyed that the last time.

"Eddie, please... Fuck." She almost falls over when I nip her tight cheek before letting my tongue once again follow the seam between them. "Holy hell."

I munch on her body lightly as I work my way to her left hip. Once there, I stop and stare at the new addition. The design is a bleeding heart with wings that appear unable to save it from its fate. I don't like what I believe this may mean. "Why do you have this?"

Angela tries to pull me away by clutching my hair and tugging on it hard. "Just something I wanted, so I got it."

I dig my fingers into her thighs and hold tight. "This is not something you just get for the hell of it, *Anjo*. Don't lie to me. Why?"

She tugs harder. "It doesn't matter."

My chin rests on her hip as I gaze up at her. "It matters to me."

There is agony in her brown eyes, it is the kind that guts me. I rise to my feet and place my hands on each side of her face. "Did you get it because I broke your heart?"

Tears build until they are so full, they spill down her cheeks. Her bottom lip quivers slightly as she tries to keep it under control.

"I'm sorry." My thumbs wipe at the tears. "I never meant to cause you this kind of pain."

"I know. I also knew what I was doing, Eddie. It does not rest completely on your shoulders. And don't be such an arrogant man. You may have been the one who sent it on a spiral, but you are not the man who started the bleeding of my heart. I do believe that falls on Ramon." She shakes her head free and turns to grab one of the many products behind her.

I chuckle as I take in the bottles lined up along her shelf. "Do you seriously use all those?"

Grabbing some scratchy looking buffer, she snags a bottle and squeezes a sizable amount inside. "I do. It makes my skin soft and keeps me appearing young."

I run a finger down her arm and hum in appreciation. "I don't believe you need all these to do that, but if it is what you like, then I'm willing to help."

"I don't think so." Angela tries to bump me away with her hip, except I refuse to budge. "Edward, there is a shower right over there you can use. I'll even let you borrow my soap." She picks up a white bar of soap and a washcloth as if getting ready to hand it to me and send me on my way.

I wrap my arms around her naked torso and tug her against mine, then lean down and place my lips on her ear. "I'm not taking a shower over there. I am having a shower here with you where I can appreciate this body that has been driving me crazy for way too long."

My teeth graze the shell of her ear, causing a whimpering sound to escape her lips before she tries to object. "It's a tedious, thorough process."

"Good. Now tell me what they call this, it looks like it washed to shore and dried in the sun." I accept the rough buffer and run it over my palm, it's very scratchy. "You use this on your delicate skin?"

Angela goes to reach for it, but I hold it higher than her ability allows. "It helps exfoliate the skin, cleans off the dead, opens the pores, allows the new to shine."

I take a step backward and snag one of her arms. Gently, I begin to run it up and down her skin, taking my time. Making certain I get it all before moving on to another body part. When it is time to scrub her legs, I am back on my knees making sure I do a proper job.

"I believe this is below your paygrade, Captain. It is your duty to protect me, not wash my body." She sighs when I lift one of her feet to make certain they too get scrubbed. "Have you done this before?"

I shake my head as I spin her around and work my path up her backside. She gathers her dark hair and draws it over her shoulder so it is not in my way. When I'm satisfied, I hand her the scratchy item and kiss her shoulder.

"What is the next step?" I feel her quiver. "And you are wrong. Official body washer is an upgrade from being your protector. It is my pleasure to adore this body the way it should be adored. So, what is next?"

She hands me something in a plastic jar. "Tonight is the night I use the sugar scrub to help soften my skin. You just spread it all over using only your hands. Well, not all over, I don't put it down there."

"I am liking this job better and better." I dip my fingers into the jar and begin rubbing it all over her glorious curves. When I reach her arse, I take my time, kneading it just right. I spin her again and paint it all over her front, making sure to get her breasts extra good. Forcing them to peak to a point that has my cock aching and my lips longing to touch them. "Are you positive your pussy doesn't need a little sugar rubdown?"

Her lips curl upwards. "I'm certain."

I don't argue. My job is to wash her day away, and that is what I am doing. It is by no means a hardship for me. "Now what?"

She steps under the shower and lets the water rinse her off. I was expecting her to hand me another one of the bottles. Instead she grabs the soap and washcloth, rubs the soap into it, and then gets to work on mine. "Now it is my turn."

I spread my legs and let my arms drop to my side. "Her Royal Highness has now become the body washer to the Captain of the King's Guards. That, Madam, is a job below your status. Are you confident you wish to lower yourself to such a task? I'm not a small man."

Angela scrubs more soap into the washcloth and then washes my shoulders. "If you are going to sleep in my bed, Sir Edward, we must make certain you are clean from head to toe." Her hand runs down my chest, catching the suds sliding down it. She rubs them in and then travels further south, down my abdomen to the coarse hair just above my extremely hard, throbbing cock.

"Fuck," I growl. "You are playing with fire, *Anjo*. I will fuck you in this shower if you get me too worked up."

Raking her nails across my lower midsection, she toys with me. She washes me thoroughly with her other hand while teasing, but not touching me there. Drops to her knees, even, and I cannot help but watch her. My mind imagining her lips wrapped around my now weeping member.

I breathe again when she stands, thinking I just might survive this when the minx surprises me by grabbing on tight. "A large man indeed."

"I'm going to fuck you so hard you will ache for days," I warn her as I walk us under the water so I can rinse off all this soap. My lips find hers as she continues to stroke me until I can no longer take it anymore. I grab her hand to stop her. "Oh no, you don't. When I come, it will be when I am so deep inside of you there will be no other choice."

I rinse us fully, kissing her while I do. Turn the spray off and shuffle us toward the towel rack where I snag two large ones to dry us. As I'm wiping the water from her, she begins to do the same to me.

"Edward, this may seem like an odd question, but bear with me, will you?" Her eyes lift to mine and I see how serious she is, so I nod. "When was the last time you slept with someone?"

My body stiffens because this is a topic I was not prepared to discuss with her. At least not yet, I realize we might eventually talk about our past lovers.

"I'm asking because, in all honesty, it's been a while since I have entertained a man in my home. I don't have the proper supplies." Her cheeks redden. "And I've only ever not used a condom with Ramon."

I tug her close as I take in her words. Funny how I'd not thought ahead either. While I have a condom on me at all times, it hasn't been replaced in a while and is possibly outdated. "It's been almost a year."

She makes a face and I know why. My last relationship—if you call it a relationship when you only fuck a woman for the weekend and then move on—was with someone she is not fond of. A woman who was more than happy to share our brief fling with Angela, as if rubbing it in her face.

"Don't." I let my forehead rest against hers. "One fuck, one night. I do not care what she disclosed to you. It was a quick, brief, and a less than satisfying encounter. Your turn."

"A few years. No one you know. An abrupt, swift affair. And nothing was ever very satisfying after you. I finally stopped trying to find something I could not, instead I invested in a vibrator that gave me more than anyone else ever could." She bites her lips together, holding back a smirk.

"Anyone but me, you mean," I challenge her.

"That is still to be determined. If you cannot do the job, I have it handy to help me get it right." This time she laughs when I growl.

"I am going to make that toy obsolete and not worth your time." I kiss her hard before I pull back and ask, "Are you sure? We are not young and I'm presuming you are not on birth control."

Now she outright laughs at me. "Eddie, I had my tubes tied shortly after Gabriela was born. I was not chancing another child with Ramon, or any other man for that matter. Four little ones were more than enough for me." Then a sad expression crosses her face, as if she has just now realized I myself am not a father and never will become one. "Oh, Edward. I'm sorry. How insensitive of me."

"I'm an old man, *Anjo*. My time to father a child has long passed. I accepted that fate many moons ago."

"You would have been a wonderful father. Over the years you've stepped in when my children needed a little guidance from a man. I'm sorry you never got to know how that felt. That you lost..."

I put a finger over her lips. I don't want to hear her sympathy for what I lost. I know what I lost, a wife and child. It took me years to move past that, to forget what it feels like to love someone and then lose them without warning. It was the reason I kept all my relationships short and unattached. Now, however, I think I might want to remember what it is like to be attached and fall again.

"Let me love you, *Anjo*. I want to if you will let me." I whisper against her lips.

She answers with a kiss, one that leaves no room for misinterpretation. I scoop her in my arms and proceed to carry her to the bedroom so I can do just that.

CHAPTER 10
Angela

The Royals

Thirteen years is a long time. I thought I remembered all there was to remember about the man hauling me off to bed. I was wrong.

His body is more beautiful than I recall. Edward was always a fit man, but for some reason, he seems a little more now. The thick whiskers that line his jaw are now a mixture of white and reddish brown. His mop of auburn hair is still full and wavy. It is often worn loosely, giving him that just fucked appearance I've always found sexy.

The man is a sex god, and so many of the women in my circle have admired him openly. If they only knew how amazing it was to be under him when he took over and owned a woman's body. A few I guess have, and it killed me to hear them chatter about it. If I have my way, none of them will get that chance again, not this time.

It is getting late and the yawn that escapes me has him pausing. "You've had a long day."

"As have you, but that does not mean I want to stop and forget about the pleasure you promised to bring me." I yawn again and curse my body for not playing along with my desire to have this man.

Ever the gentleman, Edward tugs me up the bed and then tucks me under the sheets next to him. Both of us are naked, so it would be very easy for me to entice him by grabbing his hard dick and giving it a few decent pulls.

"Stop it or I'll leave." He swats at my hand and then flips me over so my back is now to his front. "I cannot have you tired."

"Eddie, I am tired most of the time." I yawn again. "Are you seriously not going to fuck me? I need a worthy orgasm so sleep can take over."

A few complaints are murmured into my hair before I am flipped onto my back with a man hovering over me. "One orgasm, then you will sleep."

"One is all I usually ever get offered, anyway." I squawk when he pinches my clit, nearly sending me into one right then. "Oh god, you are going to kill me."

A most delicious grin takes over his face as he cracks his neck. Then he kisses me while he massages the magic knot most men overlook. I'm squirming, reaching internally for what I know will come soon. Except right before it happens, he stops.

"Edward, I swear..." My words drop from my lips when he nips my left nipple just hard enough to produce the good kind of pain.

"You were saying." The arrogant arse does it again while he teases my wet folds, circling my throbbing clit, but not touching it. "Can your little silicone friend do this?"

Fuck my little friend that is in my drawer right next to me. No, she cannot suck on my breast, nip at them just right, all while torturing me. But then again, the men I've been with cannot do this either, or maybe they just haven't bothered. Most were more concerned about their own needs and desires to take the time to meet mine. It's why I invested in her, to begin with, because only a woman can find that exact spot and get it done quickly.

He is driving me to a high I've not experienced in so long. "Where do you keep the offending device?"

"What? Why? You are not destroying anything. I will not allow it." I protest as he rises just enough to reach my side table and yank it open.

His eyes bounce around in delight and I want to slap him. I know exactly why, and I also realize he is going to be a complete prick about it. "You have two?"

Shoving against his chest, I try to move. "So, it seems I do. One is for deep penetration, good at stimulating my g-spot. The other is a clit stimulator. If you fuck that one up, I'll never forgive you. It's magical and better than any man's ability."

Yes, I said it. Poked the ego of a man who takes great pride in his talent to drive a woman insane. It was intentional I must admit, done to get under his skin and have him needing to prove I'm wrong.

He picks up my black vibrator first. Pushes a few buttons, testing it out. Then rises to his knees and props himself above my abdomen, not sitting on me exactly. He glances down at his thick, vein-lined dick as if studying it carefully. Then he inspects the vibrator, dares to compare them by placing it next to himself. His eyes connect with mine, and I try hard not to snicker.

"You used this for deep penetration? It seems a little dumpy if you ask me. Not to mention lacking. I mean, if this is the best, you might want to petition for a refund." He then tosses it over his shoulder and reaches for the other. "This is supposed to stimulate your sweet spot."

"Yes, and trust me, it does a much better job than most men." I reach for it so he doesn't toss that one, but he is fast and hides it behind him. "Don't fuck with me, Edward."

"I won't destroy your special toy, promise." He slides back and places my stimulator on the bed next to him, just out of my grasp. "It's been a while since I've tasted a woman's sweet pussy."

He has such a dirty mouth, and it has me growing wetter than I have been in a while. His words alone do more than the men I wasted my nights with, and that is very sad.

"Tell me, Angela, when is the last time a man was allowed to eat this pussy?" I nearly explode when his tongue licks my smooth skin. I almost faint when he buries his nose deep and inhales. "Fuck me, *Anjo*. This pussy of yours could very well send me to an early grave. I could spend a lifetime devouring it and forget everything else. I could feed on it for hours. I will too, but not tonight."

I close my eyes and tilt my head back. This man is going to propel me into an orgasm long before he even gets started. Just the thought of all he can and will do has my legs going numb. "Edward, please."

"Please, what?" He spreads my folds and blows. "You want me to eat this pussy, *Anjo*? Suck on your clit? Play with your beautiful breasts while I do?"

I glare down at his smug face and taunt him again. "I thought you were hoping to prove something. So far you've only made me wish I had my..."

I hiss when he rakes his teeth over my throbbing clit. Holding my breath unintentionally while he does a fine job making me wonder how I ever let him go. Fucking hell, this man has a magic mouth, and I come in such a rush I nearly pass out. But he doesn't stop there, no he keeps going, reaches up and pinches my nipples, thrust a few fingers deep inside of me even. Finds that spot my damn vibrator barely strokes and has me riding his face like a greedy woman who has been neglected. I swear out loud a few times before I scream louder than I meant to, as the most powerful orgasm of my life seizes my entire body.

When I come to, he is above me smiling. "You okay?"

"I think so," I whisper.

It is then I notice he is holding my toy in his hand. "So, tell me love, which would you rather have?"

"It's a toss-up," I lie and then squeal when he flips me over onto my stomach and lifts my arse high in the air. "Edward?"

"A fucking toss-up, you say," he snarls against my back. "Fuck that shit."

I gasp when I feel him slide inside of me without warning. Suffer from him stretching me as he drives home and strokes that spot again, still not fully in. He slams home, and I have to make myself focus so I don't blackout.

"Grab your little device," he orders.

"What? Why?" I pant, trying to stay with him. "Please, Edward. Don't be such a..."

"Grab the fucking toy and put it on your clit or I will."

I find it, turn it on, place it where I like it, and am instantly hit with another powerful orgasm. It differs from the other though, not nearly as exciting. Even with him driving hard into me while my body convulses around him. When I cannot take it any longer, I drop it and start to cry. I'm not sure why, really.

In seconds he slides out of me and has gently flipped me over, a worried expression on his face. "I'm sorry."

I reach up and pat his face. "You have proven your point."

His lips fall to mine and his kiss is softer than I'd expected. I feel him slide back inside of me and this time his movements are slow and soothing. It is very clear that he is no longer fucking me, in this moment he is making love, and my heart nearly explodes at the thought. In all the years I've been sexually active, only one man took his time with me. Slowed it down long enough to make it feel like more than just a fuck. That man is this man, and I know should he walk away from me again I'll not survive it.

"Eddie," I whisper against his lips.

"Shh," he hums between kisses. "Just feel. No words yet, *Anjo*. Just feel and let it be enough for now."

So that is what I do. I allow him to take his time, feel him while he guides me to a new high. Let him show me with his actions what it is he wants to tell me. When my next orgasm hits me hard, his follows. It is so strong that I can sense each pulse deep inside, like he is spilling his heart and soul into me. Once it is over, he gets up, disappearing into the bathroom, and comes back to clean us both before tucking in beside me. We fall asleep quickly and as I doze off I wonder what tomorrow will bring when the sun rises.

CHAPTER 11
Edward

The Royals

I wake with my arms wrapped tightly around a woman. Not just any woman, the woman I have thought about for many years. The one I'd not been smart enough to hold on to the first time she let me get close to her.

Her beauty goes deep.

I've known this incredible woman for almost twenty-eight years. It wasn't until King Ramon took the throne officially that he brought his family to live in the palace. Until then, I worked for his father as one of the up-and-coming King's Guards. And like all the kings before him, King Ramon eventually picked the men he trusted most. I happened to be one of those men. And for some reason, he trusted me the most with his wife, my Queen.

For years, I sat and watched them pretend in the presence of the masses, while they let it fly out behind closed doors. I'd stood back and listened to him belittle her. Explain how foolish she was for believing in the fairytale that she would be the one to change how it had been for years. Watched him remind her time and time again where her duty laid, what her position was. Witnessed how much she struggled when he betrayed their marriage openly in front of the palace staff.

I will never forget the night I found her in the garden crying.

"Are you okay, Your Majesty?" I asked, worried.

She was wringing the life out of a handkerchief soaked with her tears. "I'll be fine, Sir Edward. Thank you."

"Do you want to talk about it?" I stood several paces away, afraid to get too close.

Her gaze remained down. "Do you know what I've just had to endure?"

I'd shook my head, but because she wasn't looking, she couldn't see, so I spoke. "No."

Her eyes found mine and the heartache in them made my fists tighten behind my back. If he'd done anything to hurt her physically, I'd have made him pay dearly.

"I've been accused of having an affair. A fucking affair. Is he serious? When the fuck have I had the time to have an affair? And what man in his right mind would dare sleep with the King's wife?" She sighed so hard her chest heaved. "Do you know why he is accusing me of this?"

"No." I stuck to a precise response, afraid I would give myself away if I said more.

Something like, *Yes. I can, because it has crossed my mind to show you what a man should act like when committed to a woman, especially one as amazing as you.* The quick answer was safer and why I always held to those.

"I'm not sure where he learned sex education, but he seems to have forgotten that it only takes one time, at the right time, to create life." Her eyes fell to her hands again. "Trust me, I am equally surprised to discover I'm with child again. It was not my plan. Not what I had wished for, to have another child with a man who has no real clue how to raise children. He's more than happy to let them be raised in the same manner his parents raised him, sees no problem

with that. Claims he's turned out fine, that his siblings all turned out fine. I'm not sure what world he is living in, but none of them are fine. They all live very fucked up, have very sad and unhappy lives. That is not the kind of life I wish for my children. It is not how I will raise them, either. One way or another I vow to make sure my children will be better, do better, expect more out of all of this than those before them ever did."

In that moment, I gained a new respect for her. Vowed to help her do just that. I wasn't positive how, but I would do my best to extend my support and influence her children if needed. Perhaps be a man they could count on; one who would offer advice, even when it wasn't always requested. Make myself available to the young princes, someone they could talk to without judgment.

My *Anjo* has done just that. Raised four astonishing children, each one confident to be better than their ancestors. King Antonio broke all the rules, went against the crowd who wanted him to yield. I may have wanted to wring his neck when he finally found Queen Larkin. And then did everything he could to win her over, even breaking the protocol I established to keep him safe. I respected him, though, and initiated the best ways to allow him the freedom to have the life he was looking for.

Prince Esteban was no better, really. He put a lot at risk while pursuing Princess Winifred in secret. Making it very difficult for my staff to make sure it remained a secret until they were ready for it not to be. A challenge all on its own, but one I have to admit gained my approval. His desire to respect her like no one in her life had before made me want to support him the best I could.

Prince Lorenzo may have been my biggest test. The fact he literally ran off with his sworn enemy's mistress and child. I'd almost gone after him, but Angela had begged me to see it through the eyes of a man in love. After Princess Violet's life was exposed by the man who held her down, it was then I understood why he'd felt the need to protect her. Admired him for doing the right thing and not caring what anyone else thought, only ever concerned with the two souls who stole his heart.

And while Princess Gabriela is still figuring it all out, there is so much about her life no one knows that makes me very proud. If I had a daughter, I'd want her to have her strength and determination. To simply be the person she is and not let the world decide what and who she will be.

The woman in my arms has stood in the midst of a tough crowd and walked against them. Pushed her way through when so many were determined to hold her back, tried to force her to do it the way it had always been done.

If I'm honest with myself, she reminds me of the first woman I gave my heart to. The one who stepped away from it all, the money, the rules, the expectations, and settled for a life of destitution, uncertainty, and hard work. Her family disowned her, never even attended her funeral. It was why when my Queen stated she wanted a better life, I understood where she was coming from.

I stroke her back, kiss along her neck, soaking in the scent of her. My cock hardens against her arse. I cannot recall the last time I woke up next to a woman with this kind of desire. It has been years since I took my time in the morning to wake one. My hand lands on her hip so I can rock into her, letting my swollen and eager member slide between her legs.

"Good morning." Her voice is hoarse. "You're still here."

I nip her collarbone as I rise to my elbow so I can gaze down at her. "Were you worried I'd not be?"

She reaches back and caresses my leg, pulls a few of the hairs playfully before she answers. "I'm not sure. I think I'm more concerned about what happens when we walk out of this room." Her arse moves, and I swear I'm getting more turned on by the second.

My hand slides to her stomach and then ventures lower until it comes in contact with a small patch of dark hair. I tug on it to get her attention before letting my thumb rub the swollen pearl just below it.

As I run my lips along her shoulder, I ask, "What do you want to happen when we leave this room? I imagined feeding you breakfast before getting ready for the day."

Angela elbows me, forcing me to back off. She rolls over and then climbs on top of me. This woman has never been shy about sex. Willing to take control whenever she wanted, but also eager to submit should I decide I'd rather be the one in control. I have no problem letting her lead now, though. It gives me a chance to admire her as an independent woman who knows what and who she is.

"That is not what I mean and you know it." She is sitting on my stomach, running her perfectly painted nails through my reddish-brown chest hair. "When did you get this?"

I glance down at the scar that trails across my left pectoral and down my side. "Remember when your ex-husband had that meeting with Viktor?"

Her eyes blink a few times and she worries her head. "When was this? You did not have this the last time we were together."

"It was right after he married Sofia." She shakes her head as if she was unaware. And perhaps she was. "Well, he did, against my advice, of course."

"Of course. What happened?" Angela asks as she leans forward and places small sweet kisses along the scar.

"One of Viktor's men thought it would be fun to pull a knife out when the meeting got heated." I groan and close my eyes when she leans down and licks the raised skin. "Fuck."

"How in the hell did he sneak a knife into a meeting with Ramon?" She slides lower and drags her nails down my sternum.

I swallow as I watch her closely through hooded eyes. "King Ramon took Viktor at his word when he said all his men were not carrying. They only allowed us to do a visual and quick pat down, so I missed the knife hidden in the belt buckle of one of his soldiers. I stepped in the blade's path as it was thrust forward, intended to do very real damage to the King."

Angela pauses and rests her chin on my abdomen. "They could have killed you."

I run my fingers through her long dark hair. "It was my job to sacrifice my life for his. My duty to shield him at all cost. I'd do the same again if a threat came to my King or his family. Put myself in harm's way to save those I have sworn to protect, no matter what."

Without a word, she lowers her pink lips so they are burning my flesh again, nips my hip, and moves lower. My cock jerks with anticipation and is not disappointed. Watching her slide it inside her warm mouth, has me biting my bottom lip hard to keep from exploding.

"That's a lovely sight, *Anjo*," I tell her as I stroke her head. "Damn, you are very good at that."

She pulls off leaving my cock wet. "You are not allowed to do that now. Do you hear me?" Then she takes me in her mouth again and does her best to distract me.

I groan, thrust into her mouth even, when she lets her teeth scrape against my sensitive flesh. Her distraction almost works. "Do what? If you are asking me to not sacrifice my life for yours, or any other member of your family, you can forget about it."

With a pop, she releases me and crawls up my body seductively. I swear the woman is using all her powers as a temptress to make me agree to her way of thinking. When her tight, slick pussy encases my dick, I would almost do whatever it is she wants, almost.

I grip her hips and begin to move with her. "Fucking hell. You feel like heaven."

Angela leans forward and kisses me hard, working her inner muscles to squeeze the life from me. "And you make me feel alive like no one else. It's why I will not let you put your life on the line for me. I cannot exist without you. Therefore, you will let someone else…"

I roll us over so I am now on top of her and begin driving into her hard. "I will not."

Her nails dig into my back, and I know I'll have moon shaped marks later. "If you wish to share my bed, then you will."

I stop and glare down at her. "Don't you fucking use sex as a way to control me. I'll not have it. If you mean that, then perhaps I should go now. Walk away before…"

Angela closes her chocolate-brown eyes. "I think…"

I wait for her to finish and when she doesn't, I shift my hips to get her attention. "You think what?"

Her next words tear me in half and turn me into a wild man. "I think I love you, and I don't want the man I love to die. I want him around to live out his life with me. Is it so wrong for me to want that?"

I grab her legs and shove them wider, holding her while I hammer into her. Forget about being slow and gentle. This is about me claiming her, making her mine, all mine. I understand her words completely and hate myself for not being able to give her what she requests, to promise her to not protect her like I've sworn I'd do.

"Would you stop?" she pants. "Oh fuck. What are you doing? Trying to kill me?"

"No. I'm not stopping. No. I'm not trying to kill you." I grit my teeth and slam into her harder. "I swear to you, *Anjo*, to do my best to give you what it is you want." My orgasm spills into her and seems to trigger hers as well. When I'm done, I collapse on top of her and don't move. "But if it comes to your life or mine, I'll die to save you because I don't *think* I love you; I *know* I do."

I pull out and walk over to where my discarded clothes still lie on the floor. Picking up my briefs I step into them and then I grab my pants, pulling them on next. I don't bother with the rest. I need to get the fuck out of here before I say something I shouldn't.

"You're leaving?" Angela is still recovering, looking amazing and very tempting. "Don't you think we should discuss this?"

I shake my head and march for the door. I need a minute to gather my thoughts and calm the fuck down. It makes me furious that she would ask me something so important like that during sex. I feel used and manipulated, not that I believe that was her intention. It was all triggered by her reaction to a scar she found, one that looked worse than it was.

Sure, had the bloke who dared to attack King Ramon been a better aim it could have been fatal. Thank fuck the man was a poor excuse for a knife fighter and came at him all wrong, giving me and my team the chance to stop him. I only acquired the flesh wound because the arsehole started swiping at the air like a maniac. I'd not even noticed it until we had the situation under control. It pissed me off more than it had hurt.

I storm down to the kitchen needing coffee. When I stomp through the entrance, I nearly run over a very surprised, unexpected intruder. She shrieks and spills her hot scalding cup all over my bare chest.

"Fuck!" I grumble as I jolt back.

"Oh my god, I'm so sorry!" Gabriela starts to apologize until she gets a proper look at me. "Sir Edward? What are you doing here?"

I grab a tea towel to clean myself off while I decide how I should answer her. I'm not ashamed about the real reason I am here, but since Angela and I have not discussed how we wish to handle this, I leave part of the truth out. "I came by last night to check out a package your mother received. Decided to stay because it made me feel better knowing I was here to look out for her."

She has bent to mop the floor up with some paper towels.

"And you staying over required you to disrobe?" When she stands to toss them in the bin, I notice the smirk on her face.

"Why are you here, anyway? I thought you were in school." I ignore her question and move on.

"I have a break. Two weeks off. You know how it works." Gabriela turns to snag me a mug and passes it to me.

"Everything going well?" I ask as I stroll to the coffee machine. "You doing okay?"

Before she can answer, I hear Angela approaching, voicing her opinion on me walking out on her. "If you think I am going to let you walk away from me like that, you have another thing coming, Edward. I will not fucking have it, not after you all but confess your feelings while pounding into me like a man on a mission. That is not how it..."

I lift a hand to stop her. "You might want to hold back on all that right now."

She starts again, "Like hell I do, Edward. If you think I'm going to let you fuck me and then..."

Gabriela has heard about all she wants and cuts in. "Please, listen to Sir Edward."

Angela's head whips around to where her daughter is standing, looking very uncomfortable at the moment. "What are you doing here?"

I grab my coffee and begin to make my exit. "I'm going to go get dressed and head back to the palace."

"We will talk in a minute," Angela informs her daughter. "Edward, so this is how it is? You're just walking away. I never took you for a coward."

I face her again. "I'll be back, *Anjo*. Tonight, I'll be back to have it out with you, if that is what you want. But I have work to do, need a change of clothes even. Plus, I need to think. Thinking around you is difficult, distracting. I believe I said I'd do my best to give you what you wanted, now I need to figure out the best way to achieve that."

She slowly makes her way to me. "Did you mean what you said?"

I glance at the doorway behind her where her daughter is watching us. "Did you?"

"Yes." She blushes, now close enough for me to grab her, so I wrap her in my free arm. "I love you."

That might seem like an odd confession so soon, but I think we have both felt this way for many years, we were foolish for thinking it would pass. I lean forward and kiss her softly. "I love you too. But Angela, you will not use sex to get your way. That is not how it works. Nor will you make demands you know I cannot possibly agree to. I know exactly what it is like to lose someone you love."

"I'm sorry." She not only sounds sincere but looks it.

"I know, which is why I am going to see how I can appease your request. I need to go, and you should go talk to your daughter. I'm sure she has many questions. I'll see you later." I kiss her again, hard this time, not caring who is watching. "I love you."

"I love you too." Her words warm my heart and make me want to give her the world.

It's crazy, I know, to want to give a woman like Angela the world because to most it seems she already has it. But that is the thing those looking on don't comprehend. While she has much, she is missing the one thing so many others take for granted. I'm hoping to help her find it and keep it. Show her that she was not only fighting for her children but herself as well. That she, too, deserves to find love, real genuine love that I believe she's given up on finding.

CHAPTER 12
Angela

The Royals

I walk back to the kitchen where my daughter is standing, regarding me with very curious eyes. Gabriela and I are fairly close, the only two females surrounded by very overshadowing men. Everyone was always watching her brothers, especially Antonio and Esteban. They were the future heirs who would one day be in charge of this great country. So, maintaining a low profile was difficult, even though I did my best to protect her.

"Are you going to explain all that?" Gabriela doesn't wait, I didn't really expect her to.

"There isn't anything to explain." I grab a mug and wander over to the coffee machine. "What are you doing home?"

"I'm on break. I told you this last week, but it seems you forgot." She takes a seat at the counter and watches me closely. "Sir Edward and you are like... a thing?"

I don't miss the uneasiness in her voice, as if it took all she had in her to believe her mother was capable of such a promiscuous act. "Is it so hard to accept that I might have a romantic relationship?"

Gabriela closes her eyes when she answers. "You said he fucked you. I cannot even believe I heard that word come out of your mouth."

I have to hold back a smirk and try not to laugh at her. She's not wrong, I don't often speak like I have been. I usually control my tongue and choose my words carefully. The stress of everything going on, along with my comfort level around Edward, seems to have made me a little loose lipped.

"So, did he? Is that all this is?"

I have to give it to my daughter for being so persistent. I walk over and take a seat next to her. "I believe there is more to it than that. Some years back we had a quick affair."

"Is he the man father thought..."

I interrupt her. "No. It wasn't that long ago. It happened during your trip to France with your father. The one he took you on when you turned ten."

"Wait? So, you two have been... you've been bonking since I was ten?"

This time I do laugh, more at the face my daughter makes. "No. It was short, and it was over before it got too serious."

She throws up her hands and agitates her head. "Wait, a freaking minute. Are you saying you had like a one fucking night stand? Oh my god, you are. Is this something you do regularly? Who are you and what have you done with my mother?"

I wait for her to calm down before I respond. "Should we start discussing your dating life?"

Gabriela blushes and stares down at her coffee. "Point made. So, is he going to be my new daddy?"

I smack her arm, and she giggles. "I doubt it. I'm not sure I'll ever get married again."

"Why? Everyone, including you, deserves to find that one person who makes them happy."

I want to ask her if she thinks she is part of everyone because I know for a fact she doesn't believe she can make someone happy. My heart bleeds for her and the burden she carries. I wish I could have prevented it, taken it away from her, but her journey was to travel down that road for some unknown reason.

"Mom, please do not look at me like that. I realize what you are thinking."

I take her hand in mine. "I just want you to be happy, Gabriela. To find who you are and where your place is in this world. I believe you have one, that God has a purpose for you. Otherwise, he'd have taken you from us long ago."

When Gabriela was three, she got very sick. Her father and I learned she had leukemia, an aggressive form that refused to cooperate with the chemo they were giving her. The only way to save her little life was to replace her bone marrow with new. I had to force Ramon to get tested. He was such an arse, still adamant she was not his. The test came back that he was a perfect match; the only one in our family who could donate, giving her the best chance to fight this awful disease. The doctors were wary about using unrelated marrow because of how difficult treatments had been on her tiny body. They wanted to lower the chance of rejection, hopeful it would make her recovery quicker and she'd become stronger, faster.

I'm not sure how we kept the public from knowing exactly what was going on with Gabriela. They knew the little princess was sick, but they did not realize how sick. We were allowed to maintain some of our privacy by using the infirmary located inside the palace. Nor were they aware of the fact King Ramon was about to save his own child's life by donating his bone marrow. We hired the best doctor's we could, set up sterilized and isolated areas to keep her safe; asked family members to donate blood to make certain she had it when she required it. Being allowed to keep most of her treatments within the palace walls was the only thing that kept the press from learning how close we were to losing her a few times. Being able to focus on her care, instead of having to answer to the public helped our family stay strong.

It was Ramon, surprisingly, who did not wish for it to go public. He was the one who made certain we were set up with private doctors and tight security. To this day, I don't really know why. All I can figure was that for some reason it scared him and letting others perceive him that way caused him to appear weak. Ramon hated looking weak, refused to be seen as anything other than strong.

It took almost four years after Gabriela was diagnosed for us to breathe a sigh of relief. It delighted us to have our little girl back, but we always worried at each of follow up appointments that she'd relapse again. Thankfully she didn't and we were able to move forward with our lives, taking each day afterwards as a blessing. It got to the point where we thought were in the clear. Until eventually we were reminded of what it was like those four years.

Shortly after Gabriela became a teenager, her body was not acting the way a normal teenage girl's should. It was tough to hear what the aggressive treatments had done to her body, and even harder for her to understand. So many of her little girl dreams were snatched out of her hands and left her feeling damaged and lost.

"I need to tell you something." Gabriela directs her gaze back on me. "Please don't be mad."

I nod and do my best to ease her worry. "Whatever it is, I promise to fully support you."

She breathes out and then just says it. "I'm not going to go into the family business. I know Antonio was hoping I'd take your place in a few years, but that's not for me. I can't tell you what I will be doing, not yet at least. But I just want you to understand that I'm excited about it. Classes are progressing well, and if I keep excelling, I'll be offered a position I really want. Please don't ask me what that is, I'm not ready to share that yet. I prefer to do this on my own. If I disclose any of it, then I'm afraid Antonio or Esteban will become involved and I'll always wonder."

"I'll not say a word." I pat her cheek. "You look good. Healthy."

"Thanks. I'll be around for the next couple of weeks unless you need me to not be." She shakes her head and shivers. "This is weird. Hey, Sir Edward mentioned he was here to inspect a package you received. What's that about?"

"You are welcome to be here for as long as you wish." I stand to place my mug in the sink. "I have a stalker. Seems this person has been watching me longer than I realized. Everyone is just being cautious until they figure out what is going on."

"How long?" My daughter has always been interested in these types of matters. "You didn't tell them, did you? You kept it to yourself until it became so serious it was impossible to hide."

"It wasn't my intention. I thought it was just a nuisance until it wasn't." I glance at the clock and know I need to get going. "I have a meeting I need to make. You want to stop by this afternoon and have lunch with me?"

"I'd love to." Gabriela walks over and kisses my cheek. "And for the record, I like Sir Edward. It's weird, but he is a good man. I can tell he makes you happy."

"He does." I smile at her. "Can you keep a secret?"

"Do I want to know this?" She snickers and then nods. "I heard, by the way. It was hard not to."

"I've never been in love before, Gabriela. I'm a little frightened by it." I start to walk with her to my room. "I'm too old to be falling in love for the first time."

"All I ask is that you enjoy all your sexy shenanigans behind the closed doors of your bedroom while I am here. I have no desire to see, hear, or come across anything that makes my eyes bleed and my ears burn. If you are going to act like a bunch of lovesick puppies, I'll make the rounds to my bros and offer them free babysitting for room and board." She bumps my hip. "It's kind of crazy, isn't it, to think how all three are now fathers?"

"It is. And it seems the girls are winning so far." I smile thinking of my grandchildren. Antonio and Esteban have one of each. Lorenzo has two girls and one more on the way. All three of my sons are amazing fathers. "They would love to see you. Your brothers along with their growing families."

"Are you trying to get rid of me?"

"No. I love having you home. If I require alone time, I do believe Edward has a place of his own," I tell her and then wonder how nice it might be to spend a night with him in his own home. See where he lives and get a feel for his space. Maybe I should suggest we stay there this evening instead of returning home here tonight.

CHAPTER 13
Edward

The Royals

I've been in my office all day determined to figure out how to push ahead and detach myself from this mess. There is no way to do that, really. Even if I hand everything over to her team, I am still the man they report to at the end of the day. The one who makes the final decisions. The Captain of the King's Guards who has no business mixing it up with one of the people he is sworn to protect. My involvement with Angela is a conflict of interest and has me making exceptions to the rules I have given my word to uphold.

"Fuck," I grumble as I toss my pen across my desks. "This is impossible."

"Can I offer you a suggestion?" A familiar voice asks from my open door. "Do you mind if I come in?"

"You are always welcome, Gabriela." I lean back in my chair and wait for the young princess to take a seat. "Twice in one day, that's got to be a record for us."

"Is it?" She asks as she reaches for the folder on my desk. "May I?"

I nod and stand to go close the door. This conversation will need to be private, and while my office is in a secured area, some things aren't worth risking. "You have the proper clearance, so have at it. I spoke to your commanding officer this morning. He says you're kicking arse."

"I talked to mother after you left, shared as much as allowed. You know, let her understand I would not be taking over for her in a few years," she informs me while she reads.

"Did you do so to save my balls from your mother's wrath, or were you feeling guilty?" I probe as I take my seat behind my desk and catch her glaring up at me.

"Can we not discuss what my mother will do to your balls ever again?" She jostles her head. "I told her because I wanted to be as honest as I could be with her. It felt like the right time."

"This thing with your mother and me isn't some fling. I just want to be clear about that. That's also why I am probably struggling with how to handle this," I admit and watch a genuine smile form on her face.

She looks so much like Angela did when she was her age. Beautiful, full of life and spunk, a confident woman who knows what it is she wants and is willing to fight for it. I've watched this young woman grow up. I will never forget the day she was born; what it felt like to witness her enter this world. Maybe that is why I've taken a special interest in her specifically. Why we have a connection that differs from her brothers. There is a bond between us I believe was formed that day.

"You love her." It's not a question.

"I do." Admitting that feels really good.

"She's going to be difficult, you know. Make you work hard to prove yourself. If you tell her I told you this, I'll deny it." The expression Gabriela throws my way warns me she's not kidding. "She's never been in love before. She assumes she's too old to be experiencing it for the first time."

"Why are you telling me this, exactly?"

Gabriela taps the folder she's been browsing with her finger. "I know her well enough to realize she'll start doubting things eventually. She will assume you are looking out for her because it is your job to do so, no other reason. And when that happens, she'll try to push you away, because that is what she does, how she protects herself."

"You've seen her do this before, to others?" I don't appreciate where this conversation is going, do not want to think of Angela with other men.

A chuckle emerges from the young woman. "I don't believe the others meant anything, really. So it was easier for her to dismiss them when their time ran out. And I'm not getting into details about that, mainly because I don't know those minutiae. Mother has always been a private woman. Until today, I assumed she was also a relationship kind of woman. Seems I may have been mistaken about that, though."

"Why do you assume you are wrong about that?" It is then I realize she knows and am embarrassed about how I treated her mother all those years ago. "She told you."

"I have one question, and then I never want to talk about this again." She shuts her eyes as if gathering her thoughts. "Why did you fuck her back then if you weren't willing to be the man she needed? And are you prepared to be that man now? If you're not, then maybe you should walk away before my brothers learn what I've learned and one of them takes your head."

"Your brothers do not scare me, Princess," I counter because it is true.

Her face takes on an entirely different meaning and I realize this young woman is going to be a force to be reckoned with one day. "First, never call me that. Second, it's not my brothers who you should fear. While they hold a great deal of power and could make your life miserable, that is about all they would do. So, let me just get right to the point and give you something to think about. Should you hurt her, they will never find the body to take your head."

Pride swells up inside of me as I stare at her in awe. "Duly noted."

"Now that we have that business taken care of, let's talk about this. You are looking for a way to back off, correct?" She pauses, and when I nod, continues. "Why not take a leave of absence? You surely have vacation time built up and could afford to do just that. It would accomplish two things. You could stick to her side like glue. Drag her off with you even, for a much-needed holiday. And while you are away, the person who steps in for you would be the one calling the shots. Plus, let's face it, even if you take a leave of absence, it doesn't mean you can't stay updated. Your men are loyal to you and will make sure you are well informed. And then your duty to keep this professional no longer interferes."

"And what am I to do when it's all over? Become the Captain of the King's Guards again, only to find myself right back in the predicament I am in now? Involved with a person under my protection, breaking the number one rule that states crossing that line is grounds for dismissal." I slump in my chair, back to where I was when she walked in.

"How long have you been doing this job?" Gabriela has this expression on her face that concerns me.

"Almost forty years. I started training when I was seventeen. One of the youngest recruits to be accepted into the program." I'm not sure where she is going with her question.

"And in the forty years, you've done what exactly? Sacrificed your personal life, the chance to have a family of your own, for what? The satisfaction of knowing the arsehole King you gave a good number of the years to was not worth your sacrifice. You and I both know my father took full advantage of your devotion to him, sent you to do his dirty work more than once because he was a coward. You even allowed him to keep you from the woman you could have been spending your nights with because of that loyalty. You are about to allow it to happen again.

"Loyalty is a great quality. My family appreciates your sacrifice. Now it is time for you to decide what is more important to you. Will you choose the job that leaves you tired, stressed, and lonely? Or will you accept a life where you can have someone to go home to at night? You may still be tired and stressed, but at least you won't be lonely. Second chances come around once; they don't make third and fourth appearances." Gabriela stands and slaps the folder on my desk. "Don't forget what I said earlier. I've been paying extra attention in those classes about disposal and how not to leave evidence behind."

A laugh rolls out of me and takes over while I watch the bravest young woman I know walk out of my office. She had given me a great deal to think about.

CHAPTER 14
Angela

The Royals

My desk phone rings and I recognize by the distinct chime who it is. "Hello, Antonio."

"Why is Sir Edward stepping down as Captain?" He doesn't bother saying hello.

"What do you mean? When did he do this?" This is news to me, and I'm as equally shocked as my son.

"I just got off the phone with him. He alleged that there is a conflict of interest that is keeping him from doing his job properly. Discussed how he first considered taking a leave of absence while he took inventory of it all and determined how to resolve it. But after much deliberation concluded that the conflict would not go away, and he was only putting off the inevitable. So he gave me his resignation, effective immediately, and then provided me with his recommendation for his replacement. He claims he will have his office cleaned out by the end of next week and move out of the guards' quarters by the conclusion of the month. Sooner if he can secure a new place. What is going on?" I'm not sure my son even took a breath while spitting it all out. I can tell this news upsets him. Edward is his most trusted confidant, a man he has gone to more than once when he required guidance.

"It sounds like he's given this much thought. I'm confident it wasn't a simple resolution for him to make." I am still shocked and doing my best to maintain my composure.

"Can you go and speak with him about it? See if there is something that can be done to keep him from leaving." Antonio sounds stressed and I feel for him. "I don't understand what it could possibly be. It makes little sense to me."

"I'll talk with him, of course, but Antonio, I'm not sure it will help." Why would he make such a rash decision without talking with me first? "Sir Edward doesn't make decisions without weighing every scenario possible. If he says the conflict cannot be resolved, then you are going to have to accept that and move on. I'm certain he will be available to you should you require advice. He is not the kind of man to walk away." Except when it comes to me, then he seems to have no problem doing just that.

We chat for a few more minutes. I am able to talk him down and reassure him that Isaac would be an excellent replacement. He has been with Antonio for many years. Knows him well and holds the respect of the other guards. While Antonio hates losing him on his personal team, he agrees. The Captain of the King's Guards, after all, often works directly with the King and only administers the other teams. Edward stepped back when Antonio moved his office to Maximiliano Chateau in Homero. He believed it would be best to keep the main office in the palace since my son still considered Aragon the capital of Hermosa Islas.

After we hang up, that is when I allow my mind to speculate on all the reasons Edward would resign. While I want to believe it has to do with the fact he's finally decided to give us a real shot, that is not the first one I choose to focus on. Instead, my thoughts wander and go off the deepest end first. I imagine him packing up and taking off without so much as a goodbye. Allow negative energy to invade my mind and bring me down from the high I've been experiencing most of the day. I am now doubting if our exchange this morning was real, or maybe they were only words he said to keep me in check while he devised his plan to move on.

I am nearly in tears when there is a knock on my office door. Like the woman they have trained me to be, I gather my emotions and invite whoever is there inside. Then I quickly step into my bathroom, asking for a second, not wanting anyone to witness me like this. I know I need to do a little touching up, calm down some, before I'm forced to have a conversation with one of the many bureaucrats who stops by regularly.

"Pull it together. This isn't the end of the world. He's just one man in a sea of men. Sure, he's the only one who makes you feel alive, but he's just a fucking man," I advise the dreadful image staring back at me. I know for certain the person waiting is going to call me out when they lay eyes on me.

"*Anjo*, are you okay?" Edward's baritone voice echoes through the door. "Open the door."

I grip the sink and drop my head. "What do you want?"

"Open the door, please."

I yank the door wide, not at all ready to deal with what I am afraid he is going to tell me. Then the tears I'd hoped to keep at bay fall as soon as my eyes land on him. He's standing there looking so very debonair in his three-piece suit, holding a single red rose I know he cut himself from the greenhouse. It brings my mind back to a day when he found me inside trying to forget my troubles.

"It is stifling in here. How in the hell do you breathe?" Sir Edward stepped inside the greenhouse I'd been hiding out in all day.

"It's peaceful here. No children to tend. No staff who looks at me like I'm a walking time bomb. No disgruntled husband who wants to know why I thought it a wise idea to ruin his great-grandmother's china." I continued to prune the rose bush the way the gardener

taught me. Roses are one of those delicate flowers you have to take extra care of to keep them from turning wild or dying from disease.

"Yes, the disgruntled husband I just spent the last hour with." Edward picked up a pair of shears and started to get to work.

I paused and eyed at him with concern. "Do you know what you are doing? Tomas will not be pleased if you fuck up his beautiful roses."

"I'll just blame it on you if I fuck them up." His eyes found mine, a playful expression bouncing around behind them. "He will never get angry with his Queen."

We continued to work in silence for several minutes. When a thorn punctured my finger, I placed the offending one in my mouth to alleviate the pain. "Fucking thorns."

"Thorns help protect the delicate roses from predators. Roses are a tasty delicacy and the thorns keep them safe." He pulled my hand out of my mouth so he could look at it. "All delicate, beautiful things should be a little thorny."

I laughed at him. "Thorny or horny?"

He gasped as if shocked by my words and then repeated the word slowly. "Thorny. Roses do not like to be touched. The thorns are there to warn off anyone who might want to steal the magnificent flower it grows."

Edward then picked up the shears again. He went about properly extracting the perfect rose stem, free of thorns, with a red flower perfectly at the top. "In order to not get pricked, you must understand the proper way to handle it. Carefully remove the thorns first. Then cut the stem where it will not harm the rest of the bush, so it can continue producing the beautiful flower that draws all eyes to it."

As I accept the rose in his hand now, I bring it to my nose. "Tomas will not be pleased you stole from his bush again, Sir Edward."

He leans forward and places a kiss on my cheek. "Wrong.

Tomas helped me this time. I told him I needed the perfect rose to woo the woman whose beauty is hard to duplicate. The smile the old man wore while he went about searching was priceless. When he handed it to me, he did so with a message.

"Treat her with the same respect you would my rose bushes, Sir Edward, or you will wish you had. Her Royal Highness has been known to prick those who thought they could manage her without gloves on. You don't need gloves if you know the right way to pamper her. Remember that and you will be allowed to hold the most beautiful rose that ever walked the halls of this very palace."

I run my fingers along the smooth stem and blink a few times, not sure I can speak.

"Why the tears?" Edward catches one with his thumb. "Antonio called you, didn't he?"

"Yes," I whisper through a hiccup.

"And you jumped to the conclusion that I was what? Running?" He takes a step back and leans against my desk. "Not this time. Not ever again."

"You quit your job, why?" I let the doorframe hold me up while I take him in.

Edward loosens his tie and yanks it free, tossing it on my desk. Then he slides his jacket off his shoulders and drops it on the floor. He undoes the buttons on his waistcoat while maintaining eye contact. The fire behind those green eyes makes them glow.

"What are you doing?" I find myself asking while I watch him divest and then untuck his shirts.

"I'm going to fuck you on this desk." He unbuttons his shirt slowly and seductively.

I nearly miss his words because I am too distracted by how quickly he is shedding his clothing. When he begins to remove his trousers, I sigh in appreciation. "Why?"

Edward kicks off his shoes and then steps out of his pants and briefs at the same time. Leaving him in front of me wearing only dress socks and it is a stunning sight. His dick is standing tall and proud, making my mouth water.

"Hold this," I instruct him as I hand him my rose and drop to my knees. "You are a gorgeous man."

I then take him in my mouth and the taste has me humming. No man has tasted so good before. It's a treat that I've been craving all day, and if he thinks I'm going to stop before he comes down my throat, he is crazy.

"Fuck," he growls while I work him. "Fuck, *Anjo*."

I know he is close by the way his dick swells in my mouth. Unfortunately, he has other plans than me and pulls out, lifts me easily off the floor, and places me on my desk. My dress is over my head quickly and tossed onto his pile of clothes. He has my bra off almost as instantly, devouring my breasts as if it has been ages since he's had the pleasure.

The cool air meets my soaked knickers when he pushes them to the side and slides his fingers inside of me. Those fingers work quickly and spread all the moisture spilling out of me around, so when he fucks me he will slide in easier. My arse is lifted before he removes my knickers. Then my lips are met by his. The kiss he gives me is gentler than I expected.

Our eyes lock the same moment he slams into me hard. "I quit my job so that when I fucked you like this, you would know it has nothing to do with obligation or duty. That my devotion to you is stronger than it once was when I thought staying away was the best way to protect you."

I whimper when he pulls out slowly and then slams back home. "So, you did it to protect me?"

He growls as he grips ahold of my hips and drags his length along my clit when he pulls out painfully slow. "I fucking quit because I knew I'd never be able to walk away from you again. I should have done it the first time before I drove to your home and broke all the rules. I should have told Ramon the day he let you step away that he was an idiot and then told you the truth about how I felt."

Edward begins driving into me hard and fast now. Sending me into a powerful orgasm, making my body clamp onto his to hold him deep inside of me, drawing his out of him as well.

"I love you." The words fall from my lips before I can stop them. "Fuck, Eddie, I love you."

His lips kiss their way up my neck. "I love you too, *Anjo*. That is why I choose you this time, why I had no other choice but to choose you." He holds me tight against him, sweat soaking us both.

"Where are you going to live?" I ask when I can think again. "You are welcome to move in with me."

A cocky smirk takes over his face. "That could cause a huge scandal. The once admired Queen shacking up with the once Captain of the King's Guards. You sure you want to deal with all the rumors that are certain to follow?"

CHAPTER 15
Angela

The Royals

I t seems I was wrong about the man now helping me christen my office. I'll never sit at my desk again and not think about what we did on it. Not just once, but two more times after the initial coupling. I'm not sure I ever envisioned a man relaxing in my chair with me spread wide before him, his face buried between my legs. It is all I can do to remain quiet so as not to alert those posted in my outer office. And that seems to only make him work even harder. Use his tongue in ways I'd not known a tongue could be used to drive me over the edge multiple times.

When my legs begin to tremble and the electricity in the air makes my skin break out in goosebumps, he picks me up and places me in his lap. Impales me in one swift move and holds me there while my entire body shudders in ecstasy. My heart is pounding against my chest so hard I can feel it. I am not sure I've experienced anything so intense before.

Edward's arms are cradling my back, holding me upright because I don't have the strength. "Do you know how long I've wanted to do that?"

Through hooded eyes, I try my best to catch my breath while I watch him. "How long?"

I'm tugged forward so our lips meet. The taste of my arousal has my body reacting all over again. I find myself licking his lips, enjoying the mixture of him and me while he grips my hips and starts dragging me up and down the length of him. I am so turned on that every movement sparks the electric energy and ignites the fire inside of me.

"Fuck." I am no longer able to stay silent. "Harder. Fucking hell."

He does the best he can, striking the deep spot, sending my head flying backward. I don't even care now who hears me, not when he is doing what I've longed for him to do since our first time together. I don't care when his teeth sink into my collarbone and he sucks on it until it burns. It will leave a mark; one I'll wear proudly if this is what I get for accepting it.

He slams into me repeatedly until he empties himself as another orgasm overtakes us. I scream so loud I know anyone within earshot has heard me. Then I collapse against him and start snickering.

"Something funny?" Edward brushes my hair to the side and kisses my neck again.

"I was just wondering how long it will take them to break down the door." I chuckle and graze his shoulder. "Who knows you are here?"

Edward stands easily with me still wrapped around him and carries me to the lavatory. He places me on the sink and spins to flip the shower on behind us. It's a good thing I have one of those in here, because I am a hot mess at the moment.

"Don't worry your precious head, love. I was very clear to those in charge of your security what type of relationship we are in." He hands me a hairband and watches me wind my thick black hair up into a messy bun.

"What type of relationship are we in?" I have to wonder what the man shared.

He performs a bow and presents his hand to me. "I believe I am the official body washer for Her Royal Highness. A job I take very seriously. Shall we get started?"

I accept his palm and slide off the counter, stroll toward the shower that has steam rolling out of it. "That is not a relationship, that's your privilege you have earned after dirtying me up. You said you made it clear what type of relationship we had, so what is that exactly?"

The shower stall opens and I'm given a gentle shove inside. "I told them I was your partner. The man in your life who plans on loving you like you deserve to be loved. Do you have a problem with that? Should I have told them something else?"

Once we are secured inside the shower, I spin so I am facing him. "No. I agree with your description completely. So, does that mean you will move in with me?"

"If you are sure it's not too soon to make such a move, I'd love to move in. But *Anjo*, if I move in, then you should know you will forever be stuck with me. I'll not move out, no matter what. So, think hard before you go inviting me to be your full-time partner who cannot so easily be gotten rid of. It would also mean coming out to your family and mine." He takes my face in his hands and places a soft kiss on my lips.

We wash each other quickly. While we do so, I consider his words. I have no problem telling my family about us, I realize I am more concerned with his. Edward has a sister a few years younger than him. I believe she is married with a few children. I wonder what she would think about her brother settling down with someone like me.

As we dress, I decided to ask him about her. "How is your sister?"

He glances down at his watch and smiles. "Good. What are your plans this evening?"

I step into my heels and do a check in the mirror to make certain I don't look like a woman who has been fucked senseless. There is no denying I've been up to something by the flush of my cheeks. I grab my makeup bag to do a little touchup work. "I have an open agenda tonight. Thought maybe I'd stay over at my lover's if that was okay with him."

Edward steps behind me. You'd think my body had not just enjoyed the pleasure of him only moments ago by the way it is acting. "Your lover has no problem with you staying over. He'd like that very much."

"So, what is the plan then? Why did you ask?" I lean closer so I can apply my lipstick.

"I've been invited to a family dinner. Erica worries about me being alone, so she invites me a few times a month. And when an invitation is given, it means she expects me to come without question or excuses. Are you up for that?" Edward looks hopeful I will be. "I could tell her I have other plans tonight."

"You just said she doesn't allow you to blow her off. We should probably let Travis know we are going out. Where are we heading?" I go to grab my phone when he reaches down to stop me. "What?"

"Don't be angry with me." Edward rests his chin on my head as he stares at our reflection. "My last duty as the Captain was to switch things up a bit. I have your team focusing solely on our current problem, running the investigation, and not providing personal security outside the palace. I've hired two private bodyguards to keep watch while they transition."

"I thought the purpose of you stepping down was to remove yourself from that obligation." I feel the anger building inside. "You just can't help yourself, can you?"

"If I am expected to not throw myself in front of any harm that may come your way, then I need to know those who will, answer to me. While I trust the men under Travis' command, a little extra security doesn't hurt until we resolve this. Two more sets of well-trained eyes. Eyes that do not report to or are required to abide by the strict guidelines the King's Guards must. It will allot you more freedom and get us out from under those as well. Previous Advisors to the King were not guarded by the King's Guards." He shrugs because he knows the reason I have been under their protection.

"I do believe the reason I have been, had more to do with my other title. I recall the Captain of the Guards not allowing an alternative, even after his preceding King tried to take them off of me. He insisted on keeping me under the shelter of the Royal Family because he considered the King's Guards the finest the kingdom had to offer," I remind him.

"At the time he was correct." Edward straightens, not at all bothered by his overconfidence. "Now the best has stepped down, and before doing so made a few changes to those once suggested orders."

"You can be a very arrogant arsehole, you know. Who are the lucky men now appointed to have to put up with your arrogance?" I should have known he'd not completely step out of the way. His need for control would not allow it.

"Two men I trust. Both were at one time under my command." He must realize what will come next because he walks out before he discloses their names.

I have to wonder if I heard him correctly. He cannot be serious. The first man stepped down only recently after he married, said it was a conflict of interest to work for the family. The second man sent my daughter into a rage, acting out after he took off without so much as an explanation. I'm not sure what happened between them, but I believe I may follow his reason for leaving even if she does not.

"Come again?" I probe as I walk back into my office. "Are you trying to start a revolution?"

"No. Look, I know they both caused some waves when they stepped down, but I also understand why they felt the need to do so." His eyes say more than his words do. "I'll handle any controversy, but I will not regret hiring them. Stew and Gino are the best money can buy, and when it comes to your life, I'll only allow the finest."

CHAPTER 16
Edward

The Royals

I didn't miss the uncertainty in Angela's eyes when I dropped the names of her new private guards. Both men are amongst the fiercest to have worked under my command. Each one had good reasons for stepping away, and while I'd love to share more with her, it is not my place to disclose those reasons.

Gino Leblanc is standing guard when I open her office door. He promised me there would not be an issue, and I believe him. Although I'd left out the fact Gabriela was home for the next few weeks. It was time for him to come to terms and man up. Face the woman who had him running around the capital city like a crazy male before his life tilted on its side. I felt for him. She had a fire inside of her that not many could handle. It was going to do her well soon, and he was probably going to have an issue with her new profession once he caught wind of it.

"Gino," I address him.

"Sir Edward. Your Royal Highness," he responds, and his face is less lighthearted than it once was. I suppose if I'd seen what he has these last couple of years, it would have changed me as well. "Are we ready to call it an evening?"

Angela walks right up to him and stands there using her very confident stance. "Hello, Gino. It's been a few years. It's as if you disappeared after stepping down. You look different."

Gino's eyes find mine, and I see the question behind them. He's not sure how to handle her. If he expects me to help, he has another thing coming. Learning how to deal with Angela will give him great insight on how to handle her daughter. "I am different, Madam. Incarceration has a way of changing a man."

"You were incarcerated?" He definitely dropped a bombshell with that revelation, and she's not sure what to say next.

I step up beside her and slip an arm around her waist. "It's a long story, but I can assure you that Gino is still the loyal man he always was. Isn't that correct, Gino?"

"Yes, I am, Sir Edward." He taps his earpiece. "Stew is waiting for us by the southeast exit. He needed to make a phone call home to check in with his wife."

Angela is on a roll tonight, displaying her very feisty side, testing him. "I'm proud of Stew for being the man Karina needed him to be. We need more men like him out there. How are you fairing with the opposite sex, Gino? Do you have yourself a lady?"

"Stop it," I warn with a little pinch to her side. "You will not give him a hard time for making some tough choices a few years back. Let Princess Gabriela fight her own battles. She's more than capable, I can promise you that."

There is a slight twitch in Gino's stride when I mention Gabriela, one the lovely woman next to me catches as well. But for now, the subject is dropped and we make our way through the palace halls with no more inquires.

Two cars are waiting for us when we step outside, just like I requested. The first one is my personal vehicle, the second belongs to Darius Falcon's private security company. The same company these two gentlemen work for.

Angela does a double take as if confused. It's been years since she has been given this kind of freedom, and I have the honor of being the man who gets to offer it to her.

I walk up to the passenger door of my car and open it for her. "This is our ride."

"Whose fancy car is this?" She asks as she takes a seat and inspects the inside like she's never done that before.

After I walk around to the driver's side and climb in, I smile at her. I reach for the aviator sunglasses on the dash and slide them on. "This is mine. Do you like it?"

Once we are buckled, I flash my lights and then make our way through the back lots used by employees. We approach the guardhouse and are waved through. As soon as we hit the main road, I open it up and drive the way I often do when I'm out for the evening.

"Slow down, Edward." Angela shrieks as we weave in and out of traffic.

I shift and then grab her leg, squeezing it. "I'll not let anything happen to you, love. Just hang on and enjoy the ride."

She reaches down and grabs my wrist. "What kind of car is this?"

I cannot help myself when I give her an answer. We come to a stoplight and I lower my glasses slightly as I gaze over at her. "The only vehicle a man like me would ever be caught driving. You may call me James Bond if you wish."

As soon as the light turns green, I hit the gas and accelerate quickly, taking the freeway entrance that will take us to the upper west side of Aragon. A suburban area where my sister and her family live. Very middle class and a long way from the more prestigious region the woman next to me has spent years hanging out in.

Fifteen minutes into the drive, she relaxes a little and begins to study me closely. "What?"

"James Bond?" Angela snickers as she kicks off her shoes. "Does that make me a Bond girl?"

I bring her hand to my lips. "You would make a fucking hot Bond girl."

"So, this is the real you?" Angela takes her time to inspect me. "This spirited man who fucks like a bad boy and drives a spy guy car?"

"You think I fuck like a bad boy?" I shift in my seat because my cock starts to harden.

"Tell me about yourself, Edward. Who were you as a young lad?" Angela appears to be getting comfortable. "I know you met Flora early in life, fell for her, but tell me more. I want to know you, really know you."

I give her what I expect she wants. Explain how I grew up here on the north side of Aragon, in a neighborhood most avoided. My father worked a factory job and my mother cleaned hotels, so money was tight, but they were good people. Never let my sister and I get away with what others in our neighborhood got away with. The King's Guards always intrigued me, and my father fed into my obsession by pushing me to become one. Sent me to military school when I turned fifteen to toughen me up so I'd be ready when it was time to apply for training. I even briefly share how I met Flora, how she captivated me. It wasn't that I didn't wish to disclose my relationship with her, it just felt odd talking about my first love with the woman I believe may be my last. Mainly, I assume, because I didn't want her to compare our relationship to that one.

"I cannot believe her family disowned her like that." Angela sighs, disappointed. "Were your parents proud of you?"

I jump off the freeway, taking the exit that will take me to our destination. "My father was very proud. My mother was always worried, probably like most mothers are. She didn't care for King Ramon, didn't want me risking my life for him."

"He was not my favorite person, either," she tells me as she looks around at the homes. There is nothing special about them or much space between them. "Did she like the rest of us?"

The fact she wants my mother's approval hits me hard. "Not at first, I'll be honest. She thought you were a little snobby."

Angela shakes her head. "I kind of was. It was complicated adjusting to this life and having everyone voice their opinion on how I should be. I've never been one to sit back and let others tell me what to do. I was always getting in trouble as a young lady for mouthing off."

"I can believe that." When she slaps me, I flinch and then chuckle. "You still do not shy away. It's not a bad thing. I have to admit, I like a mouthy woman, makes life more interesting."

"Keep talking and you may feel differently about that," she warns.

Moving back to the safer topic, I continue. "My mother, however, became a fan of yours as the years progressed. She fully supported you when you finally said enough was enough. One thing my mother never stood for was staying in a marriage that was falling apart. She always claimed marriage was tough as it was, and to be forced to live a miserable life with a cheating bastard was ridiculous."

I pull up in front of a three-story brick townhouse. The only difference from this one and the ones surrounding it is the color of the door. I climb out right as the other vehicle parks a few doors down. They will sit and keep watch, make certain nothing happens while we are inside.

Angela hesitates getting out, appearing very nervous. "Are you sure this is okay?"

I reach for her hand and tug at it. "Do you know how long my sister has been hoping I'd show up with a date?"

"Eddie, not to state the obvious here, but I'm not your typical date. I mean..."

I lean in and kiss her softly. "I appreciate what you mean. Honestly, I'm kind of looking forward to watching them squirm."

"Are we safe here?" She glances over at the men seated in the car. "Do you know how long it has been since they have allowed me to go anywhere unescorted? I guess I'm not really alone. I have an escort. A James Bond wanna be, but I suppose he will do."

"James Bond is cool. He also knows how to fuck his women well. Drives only the best cars. Owns the coolest gadgets. And never ever let's shit happen that he cannot handle." I tuck her under my arm and walk us toward the house.

The front door opens, and we are greeted by my sister who was about to say something very witty. But the double take she does halts her words and leaves her standing there gaping like a fool.

"Erica, I'd like to introduce you to the woman in my life, Angela. Angela, this is my sister Erica." I don't know if I've ever seen my sister stunned speechless.

Angela extends her hand. "It's a pleasure to meet you. I hope it is okay I came with Eddie. We were together when you texted him, and he insisted I join him."

Erica recovers quickly and accepts Angela's hand. "We always have room for one more." Then her eyes land on me and I know I am going to hear about this later.

We walk into what I love to call organized chaos. My sister lives with her son Andrew and his daughter Desirae, who is six. Andrew is a single father who has done an exceptional job raising a fireball. Currently, Desirae has her cousin Stefan, in a headlock doing her best to take down the ten-year-old. The princess Joliet, is ignoring them like she always does, playing with her baby doll.

Erica claps her hands together and orders them to stop. "Uncle Eddie is here with a guest, let's not scare her off."

The wrestlers glance up and then fall over when they realize who I've brought with me. Even the youngest citizens know her face when they are in her presence.

Joliet, who is seven, jumps to her feet and squeals. "Are you really her? I have always wanted to meet you. Uncle Eddie says you are a very busy lady and not allowed to visit just anyone. I can't believe you are here."

Angela walks right up to my niece and squats so they are eye level. "How old are you?"

"Seven," Joliet holds up her hands to show her. "You're really pretty. Way prettier here than on the telly."

"Thank you. Is this your baby? My granddaughter has a baby almost exactly like her." Angela doesn't shy from speaking to Joliet, and I may fall a little harder for her.

The other two join them and they ask her all kinds of questions, and like the amazing woman she is, she answers them. Speaks with them on their level, making them understand she is a person just like them.

"What the fuck, Eddie?" Erica grumbles in my ear as she tugs me into the kitchen. "Is this some kind of practical joke? Did Tonia put you up to this? Oh my god, please tell me you are not dating that woman."

I should be offended by her doubt that Angela and I are together, but I'm not. "I am really dating her. In fact, I quit my job today so I could do just that."

"Dating who?" Tonia steps into the kitchen. "Who's the woman chatting it up with the children? I don't think I've ever seen them so quiet or well-behaved."

I kiss my sister's oldest child on the cheek. "You look well. Feeling better?"

"One day at a time," Tonia tells me as she peeks around the doorway. "Holy fucking hell! What is Her Royal Highness doing in our sitting room?"

Erica responds for me. "Eddie brought her with him. Apparently, he is dating her."

"Fuck a duck. You are not." Tonia shoves me. "The ex-Queen is your girlfriend? Do you have a magic cock or something?"

I shrug and then start to laugh. "What can I say? It's my charming personality that draws them to me."

"Draws who to you?" Angela steps into the small space. "I'm sorry to interrupt. Would it be possible for me to use the lavatory?"

I point to the hallway behind us. "Third door on your right."

Erica takes off in front of her, explaining how she should make sure it's cleaned before allowing a woman of her status to use it. My sister is likely to have my head for not at least warning her I was bringing company.

"Mom's going to cut you," Tonia chuckles. "So, what is really going on? You aren't dating her. This has to be some undercover secret spy thing, right? A way to keep her safe from some lunatic."

When I don't answer, my niece drops into one of the kitchen chairs and points to the one next to her. I lower myself into it and wait for her to start the interrogation. I can see the wheels inside her brain spinning.

"You." She pauses and shakes her head. "Her." This time she scratches her face and runs her hand over it a few times. "You two are really..." She makes a gesture with her fist that is a little vulgar. "Since when? How long? Is this serious? You quit your job? Does that mean you will be a part of the Royal Family? Does that mean I have to act like a proper lady? Will I get to meet Queen Larkin? She's amazing. How about Princess Violet? I hear she's a real kick in the pants. I've met Princess Winifred, as you already know, stopped by her bakery when Prince Esteban was manning the counter. Swoon, that bitch is so fucking lucky. I cannot believe you've kept this quiet. How could you keep this quiet?"

"Are you done?" I snicker.

Tonia nods and then giggles. "I cannot believe you brought her here."

———

DINNER WENT OVER WITHOUT A HITCH. After the initial shock, my family settled down. They may have stared at her in disbelief more than once when they thought she wasn't looking, but they were civil. Even my nephew didn't make a huge scene when he showed up late. He did a double take, shook his head, and before he took his seat, he gave me a fist bump.

We didn't stay as long as I normally might. No late-night movie or nasty game of canasta. I wasn't ready to let her see how ruthless the women in this family truly are. As soon as they passed the cards out, her status would no longer be a problem, and they'd take her down. We made our escape once dessert was over. Said our goodbyes before they dragged us into a war.

"You have a lovely family, Eddie," Angela informs me as she stares out the window. "Very lovely."

"Thank you." I flash the lights and take off. "You made a wonderful impression."

"I scared the shit out of them." Her gaze flickers my way momentarily. "Your sister wanted to skin you alive."

She's not wrong, but it all worked out and this way they were authentic instead of putting on a show. They had no time to prepare to pretend, they could only react in the manner they always do. And just as I had suspected, Angela did all she could to make them feel at ease around her.

"Do we need to stop by your place to pack an overnight bag?" I reach for her hand.

"Probably would be nice. I have clothes in my office but not the kind of clothes I like to relax around the house in on a

Saturday." She places her other hand on top of mine. "Are you really moving in with me?"

"Do you honestly want me to move in with you?" I take a different route since we are heading to her home first.

"Yes." Her answer is quick. "Yes, I do."

CHAPTER 17
Edward

The Royals

I'm making the drive to Homero today at the request of King Antonio. I knew I would have to do this eventually and am prepared. Angela wanted to make the trip with me, but her schedule wouldn't allow it. So, I'd left her in bed, thoroughly fucked.

We spent the entire weekend together. Packed my small one-bedroom loft and then moved my belongings to her place. I don't own much. The lofts come furnished, and that was good enough for me. Most guards only live in them when on duty or during those early years. Since we hold odd hours, shifts extending days rather than set hours each day, we assign every guard a loft to sleep and freshen up in. Only the younger unattached guards live there full-time, me being the exception. I had no reason to live anywhere else, my life centered on my job, not the other way around. I only spent my nights away when I was involved with someone, and those were always temporary affairs. None of them ever lasting longer than the required time off every guard was expected to take.

I arrive at Maximiliano Chateau around eight in the morning. A habit that will be hard to break, getting up before the sun. I normally had to go over the tapes from the night before. Studying agendas, reports, the guards' schedules, plus any other business that required my attention. It was easier to complete while everyone was still waking. Now that I am no longer responsible for any of those things, it's going to take some time for me to adjust to my new unplanned life.

Alejandro greets me at the front door with an expression that tells me it is going to be a long day. "Sir Edward, good to see you."

"Is it?" I step inside and hear the family moving about.

He sighs loudly but doesn't answer me. Instead, we head for the kitchen where the family is having breakfast. It is a sight to witness, a man like King Antonio with his daughter on his lap as she shovels in her cereal while he helps his son with his. Queen Larkin is making their breakfast as well as going over her schedule for the day with her husband. She is dressed in jeans and a flannel shirt, a sign she plans on getting dirty today. Princess Isabel is missing, only not here because she is spending a few days with her maternal grandparents.

Alejandro waits for them to finish speaking before announcing me. "Sir Edward is here."

My King's eyes land on me as he orders me to take a seat with his free hand. "Welcome to the chaos. You are early."

"Old habits are hard to break," I tell him as I sit down.

"Have you eaten?" My Queen asks as she begins to put food on their plates. "We have more than enough. I thought you might be early, so I was prepared."

"If it is not too much trouble, Your Majesty." I almost laugh when she gives me that look. "I'm sorry. I mean, Larkin. Old habits and all."

She carries the plate over and sets it down in front of me, places an empty coffee mug there as well, and points to the carafe. "Cream and sugar are next to it."

I get my coffee ready and then eat. When she is settled, she takes a few bites before speaking again. I nearly choke on my food when she does.

"I hear you found a new place to live." The tone of her voice expresses she finds it very interesting and possibly a secret. "That was quick."

"Who told you this?" I cough when a piece of egg gets stuck. "Maybe not as quick as you think."

Antonio stands and settles his daughter into the chair next to her mother. "I'm taking Lucas with me to go get ready for the day. Sir Edward and I have much to discuss. I'll be down in thirty if that works for you." He then kisses his wife before picking up his son.

"You have trained him well." I chuckle as I watch the most powerful man in Hermosa Islas leave the room with his son in tow. "It's refreshing to see a man like him so involved."

Larkin picks up her coffee and sips on it. "Are you going to tell him?"

"Tell him what, exactly?" I'm not sure what I am planning to disclose yet, but keeping my relationship with his mother private seems impossible.

"How long have you two been involved? And don't be coy, he will eventually find out. Don't you imagine it would be better coming from you than someone else? Otherwise, it looks skeptical, as if you are trying to mask something. A man who steps down from a career he has spent his life doing, so he could be with the one person he wants to be with, is the kind of man who doesn't hide like a coward."

"Are you calling me a coward?" I sit back and reflect on her words. "I'm not a coward. I'm just not sure it's any of his damn business."

"Perhaps it's not. However, he will not let you just walk away without a logical explanation. So far, the explanation he has been given isn't cutting it." Larkin stands and takes her daughter's hand in hers. "Are you prepared to skip the holiday coming next week? Because I'm pretty sure all of this will come to light then, and I'd hate to have to say I told you so."

She is completely right. There will be no hiding this come next week. The Reyes family tradition of spending the day together means, unless I want no part in it, then it will all come to light. Angela's home will be the central location for her family. They come every year and since I'm living there now, sharing her bedroom, it will all become very clear.

"Fuck," I mumble as I grab my phone and step outside. As soon as she picks up, I start. "I have to tell Antonio about us."

"Good morning to you as well," Angela responds. "What brought this on?"

"Queen Larkin all but told me she knows I am living with you. She suggested I inform him before he finds out from someone else. She's right. Fucking hell, next week your family will invade your home. Unless you plan on keeping me locked away in your boudoir, then I'm pretty sure they will figure it out." I am pacing now, likely wearing a spot in the ground. "He's going to be very unhappy with me."

There's a moment of silence on her end and I begin to wonder if I lost her. "Angela?"

"I'm here," she states flatly.

"Well?" I grumble into the phone. "What do you want me to do about it?"

"Locking you in my boudoir sounds nice and all but not logical." Angela's voice pitches letting me know she is about to let me have it. "What do you wish to do about it, Sir Edward? You are the one who quit your job because you said there was a conflict of interest. Perhaps you acted hastily."

"I did not act hastily." My voice rises a few notches. "I fucking love you. That is not going to change."

"But love isn't always enough. Sometimes it becomes a

hindrance that impedes things and coerces a person to make decisions they wouldn't normally make. Later when they look back, they realize their initial reaction was wrong and the love they thought would be enough isn't." The finality of her words cuts me deep. How could she even consider that true? "It's fine. I get it. Life is messy," she continues.

"Would you stop with that love isn't enough nonsense? Do you recall what I told you when you asked me to move in with you?" One weekend and we are already here.

"Yes. But you are the one calling me, asking me what you should do about it when you didn't seem to require my advice the day you resigned. So, I'm confused on what it is you are asking I guess, or maybe why you are asking even." I hear a voice in the background informing me she is not alone. "Look, I have to go. Do whatever it is you desire to do. I'll deal with the fallout should I need to do so. Is there anything else?"

"Just one thing." I want to kick my own arse again. "I love you, today, tomorrow, and for the remainder of my life. Please don't doubt that even when I do stupid things. Know that my love for you is enough, will always be enough. I'll be back this afternoon to pick you up from work. I suspect it is time I took you out and showed you off."

"You don't have to do that." Angela sounds a little less mad. "I love you too."

"It is long overdue, my love. Time to be the man you deserve." I hear footsteps so I say my goodbyes. "I'll see you after work, goodbye."

She hangs up and I tilt my head to the sky above. This woman grounds me, makes me feel alive like I haven't before, not since a young man at least. It's too bad I was foolish and fought this. I should have gone after her long before I ever did.

"Are you ready to get down to business, Sir Edward?" King

Antonio asks as he approaches. "Sounds like you may have someone to get back to this evening."

"I do." I wait for him to step closer and then begin walking next to him. "Do you remember what it was like when you knew you found the woman who you couldn't live without?"

"I do." His voice displays the smile on his face. "I believe I frustrated you more than once. But when you find that person, you are willing to do just about anything to not lose them. So you are in love. This is what you think is the conflict that has forced you to step down. I don't see how..."

"I'm in love with your mother," I announce while he is talking.

He halts his movements and stares at me completely caught off guard by my honesty. "I'm sorry, did you say you were in love with my mother? Does she know this?"

"She does. This weekend I moved in with her. So, now you see..." The fist that lands on my right cheek has me stumbling back a few. "Fuck."

"If you think I am going to permit you to..." Antonio charges me. "You son of a bitch." He grabs my shirt and pulls back to punch me again.

"Stop it! Stop it, right now, Antonio. Have you lost your mind?" Queen Larkin comes running down the pathway. "What is wrong with you?"

"He's sleeping with my mother. I'll not have him..."

"Oh, for Pete's sake. How old are you? Are you a child or a man? Your mother is a grown woman who has raised four children. I assume she is more than capable..."

Antonio shoves me back as he releases my shirt. "He is living with her, Larkin. Living with her. This is why he stepped down because he is... he is taking advantage."

Larkin huffs as she rolls her eyes. "This is not how I meant you should tell him." She steps between us and places a hand on her husband. "Antonio, you need to calm down. What did he tell you exactly?"

"He started with some nonsense about me recalling when I knew you were it for me. Then told me he was in love with my mother." Antonio is glaring at me the same way I remember his father regarding me after he learned Angela caught him with his pants down. "How long have you been manipulating her like that?"

Larkin grabs his face and encourages him to look at her instead of me. "Hold up slugger. Now, you and I both know Sir Edward has not been manipulating anyone, especially not your mother. And it is none of our business how long it has been going on. You are missing the point and only focusing on the information your mother is sleeping with someone, instead of the fact she is in love with him. In love, Antonio. And punching the man your mother loves is not how it is done."

Antonio shakes his hand and then makes a wincing face. "He should have thought about that before blurting it out like he did."

Larkin takes her husband's good hand and leads him back to the house. "Come on, Rocky. We need to get ice on that hand. You too, Sir Edward. It looks as if you are going to have a nice bruise. I swear, men are idiots. Do you feel better after taking a cheap shot? You are lucky he didn't punch back."

I'm not sure what he says, but Larkin gives him the business all the way to the house afterward. My jaw genuinely hurts worse than I imagined it would. It reminds me of the time I found the boys slugging it out in the garden at the palace. I don't even remember what started it, but all three of them were ready to kill the other. It didn't matter that Prince Lorenzo was seven years younger than his eldest brother. He was equally scrappy and getting in a few solid shots.

"Why are you chuckling?" Larkin asks me when she hands me a bag of frozen peas. "It's not really funny. None of this is funny."

"Sorry. I was just remembering the last time I got punched by your husband. He was about seventeen, his brothers and him were arguing, and they were all ready to kill the other." I smile and then grumble. "Fuck that hurts."

"You've punched him before?" Larkin sounds disappointed.

"I did not punch him. It was Esteban I was aiming for, he just happened to step between us." There is a smirk on his face. "It was Lorenzo who got the best of him that day, though."

"Yes, it was. He was a firecracker even back then. If I recall correctly, it took two guards to hold him back." I chuckle.

There is a respectable silence before my King speaks. "So, you believe you are in love with my mother?"

"I don't believe I am in love with her, I know I am." I straighten up. "Are we going to have an issue with that?"

Larkin crosses her arms as she glares at her husband as if warning him to think before he speaks.

"No?" He doesn't sound so sure. "I mean no. No, we are not. But I don't I like the fact you two are living together."

"I don't think he asked you for your opinion on that." Larkin stands. "Can I go to work now? Do you both promise to behave?"

We agree so she leans down and kisses her husband goodbye.

"Are you going to marry her?" My King does not shy away from the tough subjects or questions. "Or are you just planning to shack up with her?"

"I don't know what we are going to do yet. I'm not against marrying her one day when she is ready. But I am not sure that is something your mother wants, and I won't force her into something like that again. Her first marriage was not ideal and put a very bitter taste into her mouth." I mean that wholeheartedly. If I never get to call Angela my wife, I'm completely fine with that, as long as I get to love her freely for the rest of my life.

"There is nothing I can say or do to make you reconsider your resignation?"

"No, there isn't." I place the bag of peas on the table. "I will not walk away from her a second time."

"What do you mean a second time? There was a first time?" Antonio shifts in his seat uncomfortably.

I didn't mean to share that with him, not yet at least. "What I'm saying is, I am here for the long haul. I plan on being by your mother's side, and I cannot do that if I am also trying to run security for this family. It's a conflict if my focus is completely on her and not the job. Which I discovered was going to be the case as soon I learned she'd been keeping her stalker a secret from me. My focus was solely on her and that is a problem when my focus needed to be on keeping you all safe."

Antonio looks down at his hand. "I believe you said it best earlier. When you find the one person you know you cannot live without your focus changes. I thank you for your service, Sir Edward. My family thanks you for the years you've sacrificed to keep us all safe. But it sounds to me that it is time for you to move on. I just need you to promise me one thing."

"What is that?"

"That you will love her the way she has always deserved to be loved. Treat her like the queen she should have been treated like, with loyalty and respect."

I extend my hand to him. "You have my word on that, Your Majesty."

CHAPTER 18
Angela

The Royals

My hands are shaking so severely I'm pretty sure my dear friends are going to notice. These ladies are very observant—nosey is a better word—and once they do, they won't let it go. I am extremely shaken up after what happened at my office.

My duty as the King's Advisor is to meet with diplomats, some that are our own and those from other countries. I am often required to travel to do the King's business, so my son is allowed to spend time with his family and less time entertaining those who demand to speak with him. Because of who I am, it seems to have been well-accepted for me to step in for him. Better than it would be for someone not related to Antonio, or more importantly because I am his mother.

Today one of those diplomats stopped by the palace while visiting our great nation. Here's the thing. I wasn't completely honest with Edward about never crossing the line. Most of the time I declined getting involved with the men I am forced to hold a working relationship with, but a few have caught me in a moment of weakness.

This one had done so more than once. He's rather charming, never came across as pushy or overbearing. Each time he gave the impression of being accepting when I turned his advance down for whatever reason, but eager when I eventually gave in. And I must admit he made me feel wanted. Ours was one of the brief affairs I enjoyed, but like the others, I ultimately ended it. That is when things turned into an interesting twist and why I'd done everything I could to keep our meetings public and brief.

I was unaware he was even in Hermosa Islas or the palace. He had a meeting with the Prime Minister, Madam Sara Gallo, who kept an office here when she was in Aragon. And because he had access inside the palace—it made it easier for him to move around this area more freely—he dropped by my office with little warning.

"Bonjour Madame Angela. Tu es toujours assi belle." Marcel LaRue's *voice echoed from my open door.*

"Marcel, this is a surprise." I had not been expecting him, and my door was only open because Rebecka had to step away momentarily.

"A lovely surprise, I do hope, Belle. I missed you and thought it was time to make up for lost moments." He stepped inside and then secured my door. I'm not sure why that bothered me, but it had. *"It has been way too long. Do you not agree?"*

"Marcel, I am a very busy woman. Could you please open the door? I am expecting someone." There was a darkness in his eyes that warned me to tread lightly.

"A lover, Belle? Have you so easily replaced me? I thought we had something special and then you just walked away without so much as an explanation. I do believe after our time together, I deserve one. It seems only reasonable when all was going so well." Marcel ignored my request to open the door and began making his way to my desk.

I had hoped he'd take a seat in one of the chairs, but that was not the type of man he was. He rounded it and rested his lean body there while he glared down at me.

140

Marcel was a handsome man. Possessed all the finer points women were drawn to. It was one reason he had eventually worn me down and I'd given in to his advancements. Sometimes it was nice not having to answer no when you really wanted to reply yes.

"This is not the time or place, Marcel." I reached under my desk to alert my team.

He seized my wrist in his hand and held it firmly in his grip. I had once thought his aggressive behavior sexy when he wanted something, but this was different. Maybe because before I'd preferred him to act that way, a little assertive to make me feel something other than what I had been feeling. Now I found it alarming.

He stood and leaned toward me. "Do not push me, Belle. I always get what I want, and what I want right now is you. You can make this easy, or you can make this difficult. I have no problem taking what I desire, even from a woman like you."

I had never felt paralyzed before. Unable to move. I knew he could overpower me easily. I could only use my words and hope they would be enough to make him reconsider. "Sir Edward would find issue with that."

"The Captain of the King's Guard?" His grip tightened before he released me. "He is who you replaced me with?" The disgust that took over his face actually had me feeling more confident.

"No." I quickly pressed the silent alarm and slid my chair back so I could stand. "He is the man you were only a place holder for. The one I was waiting on to pull his head out of his arse. Do not flatter yourself, Marcel. It is you who is unworthy, not the other way around."

He began to charge when the door to my office opened. Travis, Stew, and Gino entered, ready to do what needed to be done, making him rethink his actions by taking a step back before speaking. "Do not think this is over. We have unfinished business. Au revoir, mon Altesse Royale."

I sank into my chair and pondered his parting remarks that were translated, "Goodbye, My Royal Highness." The same words that were written on so many of the arrangements I've received. Was he the person sending them?

"Are you okay, Angela?" Cara, one of my oldest and dearest friends, asks me.

I don't possess many friends, but the three women I share a drink with once a month have proven their worth and loyalty. Lady Cara Trevone and I met during my courtship with Ramon. She was one of the only women not bitter that her King had chosen a foreigner over one of the many willing ladies Hermosa Islas had to offer. At the time she was married to one of Ramon's allies. Since then, they have divorced. Cara has remained single, very uninterested in ever getting married again. Lady Lauren Hilton came around to my side when I stepped in and defended her to a group that wanted to crucify her for leaving her husband. Unlike Cara, Lauren married again three times before she found the one who made her happy. Lady Robyn Quest is the newest member of our little group. She came about when I moved back to Aragon. Stood by mine and my family's side when both my sons shocked the country by marrying without warning. The support these three ladies give helps me get through the days that often feel lonely. Being a royal isn't all it's cracked up to be.

"I could use a really strong stiff drink," I admit. "So, what's the latest gossip?"

This is what we do. I know it sounds clique and maybe it is. But here is what you may not understand. We share the gossip to keep up with everyone else, so that none of us are caught by surprise when someone approaches us about something we should probably know.

Robyn starts us off, and it is hot off the presses. "I heard that Sir Edward stepped down as the Captain of the King's Guard. Is that true?"

The other two ladies stare at me with knowing eyes. They've been around long enough to appreciate a few details surrounding my life, even though I've never come out and admitted anything to anyone. A real friend knows things because they pay attention, and they have done that.

"It is." I grab the cocktail our waiter sets down and take a sip.

"That's all we get?" Cara blurts out louder than I hope she meant to. "Sorry. You aren't going to tell us why he decided to do this?"

I start to give an explanation when Lauren interrupts. "Who is that man over by the bar? He's been staring at us since he walked in."

I spin and once again grow uncomfortable. "Marcel LaRue, a French diplomat. A man not worth any of your time."

"Was he worth yours?" Lauren asks with a mischievous tone to her voice.

"Bloody hell, he is coming this way," Cara announces. "If I were into men, he might do."

"Are you not into men?" Robyn snickers. "I thought you only didn't trust them."

"Point made. That is what I meant," Cara acknowledges.

I shake my head, struggling to maintain my composure. I can hear Marcel and Gino exchanging words.

"Who is the new guard keeping him from joining us? He looks familiar." Lauren is staring, not at all trying to be discreet.

"Edward hired a few private bodyguards to look after me." I turn and motion to Gino it will be okay. We are, after all, in a public setting. Marcel is not likely to push his luck twice in one day. That is not at all how he works.

"Bonjour, my Belle. I'm so pleased you do not carry a grudge." Marcel approaches with a confidence that men like him hold. It reminds me of the same one Ramon had. I suddenly feel sick to my stomach. "May I join you lovely ladies for a moment, so I may apologize and make up with your friend?"

"Sit." Lauren points to the empty chair. "I do not think I like you very much."

I smile into my drink, knowing he has no clue what he has stepped into. This is why I call these women my friends after all. "An apology will not get you what you want."

"Do not be that way, Belle. I cannot believe you would dismiss me so easily for a man..."

"Is there a problem?" I know that voice well, as does my body.

"That was a quick trip." I turn and make a face when I spot the blackening on his cheek. "Why do you have a bruise? Oh, good lord, please tell me my son did not act foolish."

Edward accepts the chair Gino hands him and drops it next to mine. He then sits down, slides an arm around me, and drags me to him. "You can kiss it later to make it feel better." His lips land on mine and all three of my friends make that sound women do when they find something amusing.

As soon as he is done claiming me as his, Edward aims his attention on Marcel. "Who are you?"

He knows who the man is, I do not doubt that. There isn't a person in Marcel's position Edward does not know. This is a tactic he chooses to use to intimidate the other man, letting him understand he is no threat. Arrogance runs deep in both of these men. Only one, in my mind, can pull it off with the confidence to back it up.

"You know who he is, so please stop." I place my hand on his leg and squeeze it. "I've already explained that pushing you would be unwise for him. So does my son wear any marks after he thought it clever to take a swing at you?"

Edward's eyes remain on Marcel when he answers. "No. He was only reacting the way a son should react when a man proclaims his love and then announces he has also moved in."

"Please tell me you are joking." I only expected him to tell Antonio about us, not reveal our entire relationship.

"Wait!" Lauren snickers. "So, King Antonio punched you because you told him you were in love with his mother and living with her?"

"Yes." Edward takes the drink our server drops off. "And no, I didn't hit him back. Queen Larkin put a stop to it before it got too out of hand."

"Well, isn't that interesting? Don't you agree, Marcel?" Cara grabs his arm. "You don't stand a chance here. Never did, really. You see, Sir Edward is just a little slow. But now that he's done what he should have done the first time, your goose is cooked. If I were you, I'd bow out gracefully."

Without so much as a word, Marcel stands and walks away. I don't get the impression he took Cara's words to heart. He will never yield, not his style.

"Did you fuck him?" Edward growls, watching the other man retreat.

I glare at him as I stand ready to get out of here before he causes a huge scene. Without answering, I look for the two men guarding me and begin to walk out.

"Did you fuck him?" Edward steps in behind me. "Answer me."

When we step outside, I discover my friends have followed me as well. Lauren snags my arm and locks it with hers as she guides me to the SUV standing by to take me home. "We could enjoy a girl's night."

"It's fine. I don't think that is such a good idea right now." I glance over my shoulder to see Edward standing there like he's still waiting for me to answer. "We'll catch up next week, promise."

Cara steps around to the other side and leans in to kiss my cheek. "Please tell me you are going to make him grovel. I bet he

145

grovels very well and then makes you forget why you were mad to begin with."

Robyn fans her face. "I now understand why you were so agitated when Catherine bragged about her night with him."

Catherine is a woman we all despise. She's one of those women who loves to go after the men she believes others desire. I still become upset, thinking Edward was stupid enough to sleep with her.

We all turn to look at the man scowling, I know they have questions but won't ask until I'm ready to share. "I need to get out of here before he bursts a blood vessel."

"Do you think that is a possibility?" Lauren laughs. "Men and their egos. Lord, why is it so freaking sexy?"

I kiss each one on the cheek and then climb into the back of the SUV. I was expecting him to join me, but it seems my friends decided to play decoy, and I am taking full advantage. "Let's get going, gentlemen. Sir Edward has his own transportation and can make it home safely all on his own."

Before we pull away Robyn knocks on the window holding an envelope in her hand. "Sorry, I forgot to give this to you. It got mixed up with my mail. I'm not sure how, but instead of sending it back, I thought I'd just bring it to you. Have fun later."

I take the envelope and set it in my lap as I tell her thank you. When we pull away, I flip it over. All the air in my lungs leaves them. This was no mess up with the mail. Someone likely shoved this in her postal slot knowing she'd deliver it later. The writing is the same as all the others and I know I should give this to the men sitting in the front or even wait to let Edward open it, but I don't.

I open it quickly, pull out the card and flip it open. My eyes land on a photo of Edward and me. We are in the heat of the moment, sweat covering our bodies. It takes me a second to realize this is not a new photo. This is from our previous time when we first came together. The fact my hip is missing the new tattoo gives it away. I turn it over and forget to breathe. Written on the back in bold letters are five words that make me pause and think of all the ways to keep him safe.

His time is running out.

CHAPTER 19
Edward

The Royals

I'm surrounded by Angela's friends quickly when she climbs inside the SUV. These women are firing off questions while blocking me from joining her.

Lady Cara even grabs my arm and tries to turn me away with no avail. "She needs time to cool down before you go all alpha male on her." She tugs on my arm again. "Surely you know this by now. You lived in the palace with her for how many years? Witnessed her and King Ramon have it out numerous times. Now is not the time to push her, she will eat you alive."

I glance over my shoulder and notice Lady Robyn pass something off to Angela through the window, an envelope. My mind begins to speculate what that was all about. Why is she giving her something now? Why didn't she give it to her earlier?

The SUV pulls away and I huff, frustrated I didn't get an answer to my question. More irritated that I didn't realize Angela and Marcel had once been an item. How did I not know that?

"Excuse me, ladies." I step aside, determined to follow.

"Sir Edward," Lady Lauren hollers. "It's about fucking time."

I throw my head back and laugh. I was not expecting that.

When I spin to make my way to my vehicle, I come face to face with Marcel fucking LaRue.

"You will not win her over me," he spits out in my face. "A woman like Angela..."

I grab the man by his shirt. "I don't need to win anything."

"Be careful, Sir Edward, you will lose your job if you are not careful. Have you forgotten who I am?" His smug face has me seeing red. "You are just the place holder, her chance to slum it down. It's a good thing I am willing to forgive her, she'll of course need to do a little begging..."

I don't think twice about what I am about to do. This man is as bad as King Ramon. A weasel who fucks about and uses women. I'm not sure how he got Angela, but I'll be damned if I am going to allow him to get near her again. My fist meets his face and sends him backward. "Stay the fuck away from her."

We've drawn a crowd now. I notice a few onlookers with their phones aimed at us. People are so eager these days to photograph anything they think will make them instant social media stars.

He reaches in his suit pocket and pulls out a handkerchief to wipe the blood off his lip. There is a fire in his eye as he holds up a hand to the men approaching us. His bodyguards are quickly advancing, ready to take me out. I'm not sure how I forgot about them. Maybe because I'm the one usually doing the protecting and not the person someone needs to be protected from.

"Never," he growls. "You are on borrowed time. I'll take your job, then I'll have your head."

Now it is my turn to be smug. "I quit my job. So good luck with taking it. And I'm pretty confident my head will stay put as well. I wonder, though, what would happen to yours if a member of your government learned about your little side business?"

His eyes widen in shock. Men like Marcel are never as sly as they believe they are. It has been my job for nearly thirty-six years to investigate every person who came in contact with the Royal

Family. I took my duty seriously, used all the resources at my disposal to explore every freaking aspect of their lives and anyone associated with them. While I didn't always share all the information, I kept records and very close tabs on them. Knew what would need to be done should a problem arise that required attention.

"Stay the fuck away from her or you will regret it." I spin on my heels and jog for my vehicle. It has taken me too long to deal with this trash, meaning Angela is farther away than I would like.

When I reach my Aston Martin, I glance back to appreciate Marcel's scowling face. He's exchanging words with his men, nodding in my direction. It's obvious he is alerting them to keep a close eye on me. I have no problem with that. If he's watching me, then he's leaving her alone. Because the only way for him to get near her again will be over my dead body, and even then, it will be unlikely.

I pull into traffic and work my way across town. I'm ten minutes behind them. In this car, I can make that up quickly even with the rush hour being as heavy as it is.

I'm close to them now.

As the SUV comes into view, my attention is immediately drawn to a small compact car. An untrained eye would miss it, but my eyes are very well trained and I overlook nothing. If it weren't for one minor detail that drew my eye, I would have ignored it completely. It would be so easy to disregard the details like this, details that now have me checking all the tags before I drive through the gate into Angela's home.

I roll down my window at the checkpoint and don't wait for them to speak. "Run these ASAP. I want the information on them before I pull up to the house. Then I want you to pull all the surveillance we have of Her Royal Highness, coming and going. See if that tag is in any of them. Dates, times, and places we spot it when Her Royal Highness is within one hundred yards. Am I clear?"

"As day, Sir Edward. Anything else?" the guard asks, not even questioning the fact I have no authority to be giving him orders.

I shake my head no and drive to the house. My car is my baby and Angela understood that. She made it clear that I was to park it inside the garage. So as soon as I've parked, I head for the front door. My feet are moving quickly, ready to take the stairs first that lead to her bedroom, but I don't make it that far before she starts.

"You have no right to ask me such a question." She is standing there with her arms crossed, looking rather intimidating. "Not unless you wish to discuss the women you fucked as well. Do you wish do that, Sir Edward?"

"No." I stride her way. "But why Marcel fucking LaRue?"

She stomps her foot and spins, heading straight for her office. "Why Catherine? Why Melinda? Why Jory fucking Gordano?"

I follow her and hang my head in shame. She seems to know each lady I dared to entertain, or at least the ones she loathes with a passion. "They meant nothing to me. I swear."

When we reach her office, she heads straight for her desks and flings the envelope in her hand down, then takes off for the minibar. I watch from the doorway as she places two tumblers on the counter and sets the crystal decanter down. Opening the small ice chest, she grabs a handful of ice and tosses them in the tumblers. Before she pours, she opens the small fridge behind her and pulls out a bowl of cherries, pops one in her mouth before she drops several into one glass. Then she reaches into it again and plucks out a lime, grabs a knife, and begins slicing. Shot glasses are produced next, a salt shaker, and a very expensive bottle of tequila.

Once she has poured all the drinks, I watch in awe as she licks her hand, shakes salt on it, and does what I taught her to do that night she found Ramon in bed with another woman. I watch her do it three more times before she gazes up at me. "Are you just going to stand there and watch me get drunk? Or are you planning to join me?"

I strut over to her and take a seat on the bar stool across from her. She slides the shot glass my way along with the lime and salt. Motions for me to do my best to keep up with her as she slams down another. I do just that and pour myself another since she is three ahead of me. It's been years since I've done shots, and I know tomorrow is going to be hell if we keep this up.

Angela slams one more down and then grabs the tumbler. It is filled with bourbon and floating cherries. She takes a sip and heads back to her desk and drops into the chair. Kicks off her shoes and places her feet on the desk as she leans backward and stares at the ceiling.

"Why are we getting drunk?" I ask her as I slam down another and grab the tumbler she poured me.

She swirls her drink, reaches inside it with her tongue and snags a cherry, then swallows a healthy portion of it. I nearly come in my pants at how sexy she looks right now. Her skirt slips up her luscious thighs, giving me a peek at the garter she slipped on today.

My cock thickens rapidly. I stand and move slowly, watching closely so I miss nothing. Fucking hell, this woman is stunning and all I want to do is worship her like she deserves. When I reach her, I rest my arse on her desk and place a hand on her foot, dig my thumb into her arch and caress it.

She watches me intently while she continues to enjoy her drink. Takes her other foot and runs it down my leg and then back up until it is playing with my balls. "I need to tell you something."

It is then I remember the envelope she threw on the desk. I find it easily, snag it, and then flip it in my hands. "Robyn gave this to you."

Angela grabs an ice cube and sucks on it. "Someone put it in her mail slot."

She is staring at it instead of me. I can see the wheels inside her head turning and know something is bothering her. "Are you positive about that?"

Her brown eyes find mine quickly. "I have no reason to believe otherwise. While I've not known Robyn as long as I have known Cara and Lauren, she's never given me a reason to think she'd lie."

"All right. So why do you look so worried, conflicted?" I tap it on my leg and wait for her to share her thoughts.

Her legs slide down to the floor. She stands and walks over to the bar again as she instructs me to open it. When she gets there, she pours herself more bourbon and sighs. Her eyes peek up to watch me as I do what she says.

I pull out the photo inside and jump to my feet. "Fuck. What the actual fuck?"

"It seems someone took a photo of us during our brief affair. I believe that was right after we rode out to the ridge and had a picnic in the field." A lovely blush takes over her already flushed cheeks. Spreads down her chest and disappears behind her blouse.

I stare at the image in my hand and can't help but get lost in her expression. It is clear she is getting one hell of a fuck. I let my mind go back to that meadow all those years ago.

"Why are you staring at me like that?" Angela asked as she sipped on the wine I packed.

"You." I kicked off my shoes and undid the zipper on my jeans. "I'm fantasizing about all the wicked acts I am going to do to you out here."

A beautiful blush spread across her body as she watched me disrobe. "Someone might see us."

I did a quick glance around the abandoned field and chuckled. "Like the horses, maybe? Or are you worried the trees have eyes?"

"I've never..." Her words stopped when I grabbed her and began working the buttons on her shirt free. "Eddie... this is crazy."

"You make me crazy," I told her as I grazed the newly exposed

skin and helped her out of her clothes. "When was the last time someone worshipped you out in the open for the earth and sky to admire?"

"Never," she replied, breathlessly.

I grabbed her foot and kissed the toes. "What a fucking shame that is. You, Anjo, should be worshipped regularly. Worshipped and fucked so good you forget everything, even your name." I watched her body shiver as I did my best to show her exactly what she had been missing.

"Holy hell. Oh shit. Goddamn, you are really great at that." Angela moaned more than once, making me enjoy owning her body like no man had ever done before. "Eddie, please."

I crawled between her legs, suited up with the condom I'd packed in our lunch, and then entered her slowly. Until that moment I'd only fucked her hard and fast, drove into her like a man determined to ruin her sweet pussy. That time, however, I had a different goal in mind. I planned to love her like I had always dreamed of loving her when she belonged to a man who wasn't me. I wanted her to always remember me like this, to be able to recall this moment when our time was over and I was gone. It had been slow and tender, painfully passionate, and burned a permanent memory in my brain and heart. And when I could no longer go slow, I started pounding into her harder until we both orgasmed. Collapsed on top of her and found myself admitting that I loved her, even if I never said the words out loud.

When my mind returns, we lock eyes. I can see she too is recalling our time together. I break the gaze so I can look down at the photo. Using my training to determine where this had been taken, flip it over and freeze.

My blood is boiling. My mind is ready to explode. Whoever this person is, they just poked the fucking bear and are about to get mauled. Like hell it is. If anyone's time is about to run out, it's this motherfucker.

CHAPTER 20

Angela

The Royals

The holidays came and went. Our family traditions have changed now that three out of four of my children are married. We spent the weekend before together, had a big dinner, let the little ones open presents.

Edward was right there by my side the entire time. My children welcomed him with open arms and didn't ask too many questions. They let Isabel, Charlotte, Sunniva, Danilo, and Nicolette do it for them.

At thirteen, Isabel was probably the most interested in our budding relationship. She understood completely that Edward was more than just my boyfriend. That we were not having a sleepover or slumber party like the other four assumed. Was even brave enough to share her thoughts on how she felt about the two of us to her oldest brother. It was obvious this topic had come up more than once, and she suggested he needed to mind his own business. Larkin had a hard time keeping a straight face while she listened. That young girl may not be mine, but I cared for her. I know one day she'll grow into an incredible woman who is going to change the world.

The other four were only interested in Edward because he was fun. He was amazing, actually. Treated them the same way he had his sister's grandchildren. Snuck them cookies to gain their trust. Let them crawl in his lap just so they could talk to him. Gave them all horsey leg rides until his leg gave out.

On Christmas day we made the trip to his sister's home and we brought Gabriela with us. Spent a few hours with his family. Laughed and ate way too much good food. It was probably the most fun I'd had in a very long time. His family did their best to act normal, but it was difficult for them to completely forget who we were. Hopefully one day it will feel more natural for all of us.

But now that the holidays are over, Edward is driving me crazy. He's bored because he doesn't have a job. And even though the men he once worked with are keeping him in the loop, they are not allowing him to work with them. He's now officially an outsider and has no idea what to do with himself. I hope he figures it out soon, or I may have to speak with someone about it.

I'm sitting in my home office when my cellphone rings and my sister's name flashes across the screen. Cora is my stepsister, actually. Our parents married when we were both young. We are only six months apart and she is the oldest, something she never lets me forget. I hear from her a couple of times a year. Her calls are consistently centered around a favor she needs. In her mind, it is my duty to keep her in the good graces of high society. It always has been since the day Ramon chose me over her.

I didn't realize it at the time, thought it had all been carried out long before, between my real father and mother, that I'd one day get a chance to prove my worth. I hadn't really been asked. It wasn't how it worked in that circle. When my stepfather heard about it, he insisted Cora, his daughter, also be granted the same chance. The game to win the prince's heart began. In all honesty, I would have been happy to step aside and let her do her best.

Mother had other plans. After I'd won, Cora did what she has always done, used our relationship to her advantage.

I hate dealing with her. But know that until I do, she will only keep calling. On the third ring, I answer. It seems she and my brother are in Hermosa Islas and want us to attend the opera with her—or they want me to attend, but there is no way I'm going without Edward. I realize this is more than just a social visit, it always is, but agree anyway. I love the opera and it means most of our time together will be about it instead of having to listen to her go on and on. She will tell me what she wants, and then the remainder of the evening will be about what is going on around us. Plus, it will allow me to introduce Edward to my friends, really introduce him.

I send a text to the ladies so I don't have to endure Cora and Corrin alone. Our suite is always open and has more than enough room for all of us. Having a buffer, support, will help move the conversation along when the time is right.

"Who was that?" I hear his voice question me from the doorway.

I look up and blink several times. Edward is dressed in filthy jeans, a t-shirt that is covered in what looks like oil and wiping his dirty hands off with a rag. "Why the hell are you so dirty?"

His smile is beautiful. "I was changing the oil in my baby. If you don't take proper care of her, she gets finicky. Now, who was that?"

"Cora. She and Corrin are in town. They've invited us to the opera." I watch his face fall.

"Us?" He's never liked them, always kept his distance when they were around.

"Well, they invited me, but where I go you go, right?" It is hard for me not to snicker at the face he makes. "It will be entertaining. Plus, I can show you off."

"What will be fun?" Gabriela steps up behind him, just as filthy.

My heart flutters. These two have always had a special relationship. I've regularly encouraged it, wanted my daughter to have a positive male role model. A man she could go to when she needed. I know she has. That they talk a lot about things she cannot or does not want to chat about with me or her brothers. I get the impression they've had a heart to heart while he taught her all about car maintenance.

Some would criticize a princess for getting her hands dirty, inform her how unladylike she was. Those who would dare to call attention to what her job as a princess is and then point out why she hasn't secured a man. I'm not one. I'd never tell her that. Telling my daughter that only makes her rebel even more, not that I think she is rebelling. I've always encouraged her to be who she is, and she has never been the molded princess others believe she should be. She is independent and broke the mold years ago.

"Going to the opera," I tell her and watch her face contort. "You should join us."

"Do I have to?" She takes a step back. "If it's okay with you, I'll pass. I'm leaving tomorrow as it is. I'm going to go out tonight with Mercedes."

"That's fine. Enjoy yourself," I tell her as she takes off quickly before I changed my mind. "Do you own a tux?"

Edward points his thumb at his chest. "Me? No. I've had no need for one in my line of work or social circle. Does that mean I can skip the opera?"

I stand and shake my head. "No. It only means I need to have you fitted for one soon. A tux is not required for the opera, but one will be required for the Constitutional Ball next week."

Running his hand over his face Edward sighs. "You plan on taking me to the Constitutional Ball?"

I'm now in front of him. I can smell the sweat mixed with

motor oil. I did not know a man who smelled like one who worked hard could be so sexy. All the men I'd ever been around worked in an office. They didn't get their hands dirty or sweat like this. They hired others to do that type of work. So this is very new to me.

Juddering my head to get my brain back on track I ask him, "Are you the man in my life?"

"Yes." He nods.

"Do you plan on continuing to be the man in my life? The one who stands by my side moving forward?"

"Yes."

I take a step forward and place a hand on his t-shirt, run my fingers down it while I speak. "Then why are you surprised I want to have you with me? It will be nice to have the guy I love next to me. Someone who will make the social side of these events tolerable. Later, the one I'll get to go home with and be able to appreciate how lucky we are. After an evening of pretending, I will be ready to fall into the man I know understands me. Figure out the best way to get us back to the happy place we've created."

"How will you introduce me?" Edward asks as he watches my hand skate over the waistband of his jeans.

"Tonight?" I let my other hand join the fun and hook my fingers into his belt loops. "I guess that depends. I could present you as my boyfriend, but that seems a little less than significant. Saying you are my lover makes it sound like I am only interested in our extracurricular activities. My significant other probably fits you best. Gives them all something to think about and suggest we are in this for the long haul."

Edward is still watching me as I tug him closer. "Significant other means I'm equivalent to a spouse. Is that how you see me?"

My eyes find his, and I see something there that scares me a little. "Do you not see yourself that way?"

The corner of his lip twitches up. "I'd give my left nut to be able to call you my wife, *Anjo*. How do you not know this?"

"That sounds painful," I snicker.

His arms encircle my back and he squeezes me tight. "Pain is not having you in my life at all. Walking around without you by my side when you are living and breathing in this same world. That is painful."

"What are you saying really, Edward?" I let go of his jeans and let my hands travel up his chest and rest them on his heart. I can feel it pounding against his rib cage and my hand.

"I'm not saying anything just yet. I'm only letting the idea of us being more than significant others grow on you. Know this and listen to me, I'll forever be that if it is all you want. I'll have you however I can and not at all be disappointed about it. But there is something exceptional about calling a woman your wife, especially if you love that woman and she loves you. I realize your experience is different and your ex-husband left a bitter taste in your mouth. I'd love to be the man that erases the bitterness and shows you what a marriage should be like, how it was meant to be. The kind of marriage you deserve and should have had."

My fists crinkle his shirt as I tug him forward and let our lips crash. I have no words right now. He's right about my first marriage leaving a bitter taste in my mouth. And my mind knows that what I had with Ramon was not what most people have or why others get married. Although, most of the couples in my social group had problems with their marriages. Being faithful was not a priority nor was love and forever. Marriage was a business contract more than it was an agreement to love and stand by the person forever.

Edward married before because he fell in love. They didn't have everything else figured out. Love was the only thing they felt necessary to make a marriage successful. I'd learned that was how others thought about it as well, those who had strong ones. The foundation was built from the love they had and the other stuff was dealt with later.

I've never had that. This was the first time I have ever been in love. It is an intense love, one I feel deep inside of me. I've lived without it for a while. Was denied it because the bureaucracy would frown on someone like me falling in love with someone like him. We'd allowed others to dictate us, let them steal away the love we could have had if we'd been brave enough to just grab it and run.

I'm not ready to jump just yet. I need time like he suggested to get my mind around this. To look at marriage through the eyes of a woman in love, instead of a woman fulfilling an obligation. But if I'm honest, I think it might be something I'd like to have with him one day, sooner rather than later. Let this man show me how different a marriage can be if it starts off with the foundation of love to hold it together.

CHAPTER 21
Edward

The Royals

Angela looks stunning. She always does when she readies herself for a night out with those who will judge her. And I hate that. That she puts on a show for them, dresses to the nines because she knows if she doesn't someone is bound to say something about it.

Earlier, I had the privileged of watching her. Standing there in her large closet in her undergarments while she stared at the countless amount of fancy gowns. Some still had tags on them. I'd learned the reason for that was because certain events required her to wear a garment that has never been worn before—by her or anyone else, a one of a kind. I'm not sure how I had not figured that out before, since I always took the time to inspect her closely from afar at those functions.

She settled for a red gown that had a slit up to her thigh and hugged her curves nicely. It was floor length with a small train behind her. I knew exactly what I had planned for that dress later.

The moment we walk into the opera house, all eyes fall on her. I've witnessed it before, understood what to expect, or so I thought. However, I had been wrong, because those times I'd been one of her guards, a person in the background no one noticed. Tonight, I am the man on her arm, making a statement about where my place is in her life. Usually I am a confident man, so it is weird to admit I feel unworthy being by her side.

"Would you relax?" Angela squeezes my bicep as she nods. "Why are you so tense?"

I can sense the sweat sliding down my spine. "You are a lot to live up to. Excuse me for being a little uneasy now that I am in the center of it all. I'm used to being the background, not the focus."

"Eddie." My name falls from her lips so easily. "Are we going to need to make a trip to a private lounge so I can ease your stress?"

"A private lounge?" I'm not following her.

Angela rolls her eyes and does a quick scan of the room. Then she turns to the right and heads for a hall I know leads to a staging area. They allow this woman to go almost anywhere she wishes with no one stopping her. Gino and Stew start to follow us, but she stops them with her hands, orders them to guard the entrance, and ignore anything they overhear.

"What are they going to overhear?" I ask as we round a corner. "They should…"

Angela shoves me into the wall and drops to her knees. The snap on my slacks is loosened and my zipper gets released before I can protest. My cock is now free and hardening quickly in her hand. She is gripping it with intent.

"Fuck. What are you doing?" I should not allow her to do this. I should scoop her off the floor and order her to stop. But the sight of her on her knees has my body only able to stand here and take what she seems to think I need.

A wicked smirk takes over her face as her eyes lock with mine. "Making sure you are able to relax the rest of the evening. I'm guessing a proper blow job will give you something else to focus on. You are too focused on who they assume I am, instead of who I really am."

Her tongue darts out and toys with the crown of my cock. I almost forget what I was about to ask her, almost. "Who are you really?"

Her fist works my shaft while her breath teases me. "Your dirty woman who is willing to suck you dry."

I can only watch as her red lips open so she can suck me off like she has done so many times in private. I want to grab her head and guide her, but there is no way to do that without letting everyone out there know what we are doing in here. So instead, I slam mine against the wall, close my eyes, and make two fists to keep my hands where they are. Sweat runs down my back now for other reasons. When that tingle sensation travels down my spine, I open my eyes to gape down at her as my come fills her mouth. I watch her swallow and smile around my cock, which is now coated in the red lipstick that once covered her lips.

"Better?" The minx asks after she lets it slip free from her magical mouth.

I drag her up slowly to my lips. Kiss her hard and taste myself inside her hot, sexy mouth. "My turn."

Before she can stop me, I have her pinned against the wall and am now the one on my knees. That slit in her dress allows for easy access and permits me to pull her lacy red knickers down her legs until they fall freely to the floor. Then my head is buried between her thighs and I'm licking her smooth pussy the best I can.

"Open for me, *Anjo*. Let me give you the same pleasure you gave me. I want to walk around here tonight with the smell of you on my fingers and the taste of you on my lips and tongue." I'm pleased when she grabs her skirt and lifts it so she can spread her legs more. "Yes."

"Fuck." Angela whimpers as her knees go weak. "Eddie."

My fingers plunge inside of her and before I know it, she is coming. I don't stop until I've got my fill and know she will suffer from my powerful finger fucking for hours. I only stop when she moans and her walls are shaking violently around them. I give her one last sweet smooch, snag her knickers that are around her ankles, and drag them back up her delicious legs. Once she is put together, I stand and kiss her gently but thoroughly. I hadn't realized I was still hanging out until I feel her shove me back inside my pants.

"Better?" Angela is smiling, flushed perfectly, just the way I like her.

"Yes. You look more beautiful than you did moments ago. Sexy as fuck and well taken care of." I kiss her one more time and then send her to the lavatory just a few paces away.

When we step into the foyer, nothing has changed. All eyes fall on us immediately, except this time I am more confident. I am not sure why really, maybe it has to do with the fact the woman on my arm knows me well. Even though I notice everyone questioning what I am doing with Her Royal Highness, I decide to embrace it and appreciate that I'm here because she wants me here.

Angela leans into me. "Now this is more like it. I love you."

Hearing her express those words freely, where anyone could hear them, hits me hard in the chest. I lean over and let my lips brush against hers. "I love you too."

We pull away just before we are interrupted by a voice that has sent me running so many times. I know Cora is Angela's sister, but I have never trusted her. She has approached me more than once about entertaining her. I've declined her offer each time. But that never stopped her from trying, which was the reason I did my best to stay busy whenever she was around.

"Sir Edward," she coos, and I shudder. "It is so nice of you to escort our dear sister. You clean up nicely. Perhaps when the evening is finished, I could talk you into a nightcap."

Angela stiffens as if she has just worked through it in her

mind, but I will not allow her to think something that is not true. "I'm sorry, Your Grace, but like always I must decline. Not to mention that..."

Cora turns her nose up and interrupts me, clearly done with me now that I've turned her down. "Angela, why don't you instruct Sir Edward he is dismissed so we can go find Corrin."

Sliding her arm from mine, she steps a little closer and slips it around my waist. "Sir Edward is joining us. As are my friends." Her hand raises and I see why.

All three of her girlfriends are heading our direction. Two have gentleman with them, the third does not. The grins painted across their faces have me smiling as well. They are obviously looking forward to this, and I'm guessing it has to do with me. It's not every day a man like me leaps into high society the way I have.

"Ladies." I nod as they approach. "Nice to see you again."

Lady Lauren snuggles up next to her husband. I've seen him around but know little about him. One of the less noisy gentlemen, a man who keeps to himself, mostly. I shake his hand and then catch how he does a quick glance in Angela's direction. Notice the expression behind his eyes even if it is brief, I notice, and I don't appreciate it. His eyes shift and find mine. At least he appears guilty for pondering on matters he should not be. I doubt he'll do that again since he knows I'm on to him.

Lady Robyn's husband, however, is not as sly about it. He is appreciating Angela openly, so openly I don't miss when his wife notices. It is also when I see a flash of envy take over her facial features. She glares at both of them as if plotting, and I wonder if there is more to the envelope she gave Angela a few weeks back. Her glare lands on another woman when her husband's eyes wander that way. Maybe her look has more to do with her husband's wandering eye than anything else.

It is the third woman, Lady Cara, who catches me completely off guard. She walks right up to me, winks, and places a greeting on both of my cheeks. She is a tall woman. A little over six feet, taller in her heels. So placing a peck on my cheeks is easy for her, even though I am nearly six foot four.

"Good evening. I hear you've already snuck her off into one of the alcoves." She tsks and then laughs. "I do believe I like you, Sir Edward. It's about damn time this one had some good old-fashioned fun."

"Stop." Angela grabs her friend's arm and drags her into a hug. "Leave him alone. He's new at this and I wanted to make sure he didn't bow out the next time."

Cora misses nothing. "What's going on? Please tell me you are not... involved with him. Oh, my dear sister, you are better than that, so much better."

I know it shouldn't bother me, but it does. My mouth fires off before I can stop it. "What's the matter, Your Grace? Does it irritate you more to think I have standards you don't fit in? Or are you suggesting I'm only good enough for a romp and nothing more?"

"Edward, enough," Angela warns.

"What? I'm just confused. I mean, you heard her earlier. She's been after me for years. So it implies she is okay with me fucking my way around this crowd. I am just not respectable enough for more than a proper fuck, not marriage material."

Yes, it seems I went there. Right in front of them all, I went there after I told her earlier I'd be happy to have her however I could. One suggestion from her sister seems to have proven that wrong. It bothers me more than it should, I realize this. But Cora's words hit me in my soft spot and have me wondering if Angela felt the same.

Arms crossed, Angela gives me a look I've seen her offer others. "Are you finished?

I shrug. I know she's pissed, but what did she expect? Me to stand here and take that shit from Cora? I've always voiced my thoughts on matters, and she knows this. It got me in trouble more than once with King Ramon when I told him what I thought about the way he treated his wife. She had to step in a few times to keep me from getting fired, or worse, tossed into the slammer after punching him.

Juddering her head in disgust, she walks away and everyone follows, me included. While she walks, she talks to Cora, who is to her right. I, however, hang back, missing her on my arm, feeling more like I did before I became a part of her life. And I hate it, hate that I've put distance between us.

"Cora, I suppose you mean well, but here is the point." Angela glances over her shoulder and the spark in her eyes burns me. "Edward and I aren't interested in explaining ourselves. We don't care what everyone thinks. Nor do we need others to approve of this relationship. If you have a problem with that, then that's on you. And should you feel the need to voice your opinion, then you are wasting your words and time. I've made my choice. I appreciate where my future lies. Know who I love. One fact I've learned is that love changes everything and makes you willing to do just about anything. Even cut those out of your life who don't get it. Do you understand?"

The threat of being cut from Angela's life has Cora singing a different tune. "I didn't realize it was love."

When we reach the staircase that leads to the second floor, Angela stops and waits for me. "Well, now you do. You can share that with Corrin too. We are going to head for the suite, we'll see you there soon."

I offer her my arm again, and she takes it. "I'm sorry."

"Are you?" Angela glances at me with knowing eyes.

"No." I take my time leading her up the stairs. "Thank you."

"For?" She asks as we approach the second level.

"Giving it to her straight. Not leaving room for others to get in our way. That means a lot to me," I tell her.

When we arrive at the door to her suite, I look back down the hall. There is a third man with Cora and Corrin, a man I don't recognize. "Who is that?"

Angela takes a moment to peek down the hallway and shakes her head. "You have got to be fucking kidding me. Seems he might be the reason my siblings called. That's Lord Jamie Baresi, he's a family friend."

Before I can ask more, Angela steps inside and heads for our seats. I give it a few more minutes while I watch the three of them closely. They seem to be having a very heated conversation. The man with Cora and Corrin appears rather upset.

His eyes lock with mine and it is then I begin to understand. I'm not part of his plan for the evening. I am a nuisance he would like to get rid of.

So, this is why her sister wanted to dismiss me. Well, fuck that. Even if Angela and I weren't together, there is no way in hell I'd let that man anywhere near her. No way.

CHAPTER 22
Angela

The Royals

My heart is racing inside my chest. I cannot believe this. What the hell are those three conspiring now? The last time they brought Lord Jamie with them, it went south very quickly. I remember sitting in my home in Prieto, not sure I was hearing them correctly. Nor could I believe they thought I'd agree to their ludicrous idea. I mean, I'd gone that route once before, there was no way I was about to do it again.

"What do you say, Angela?" Lord Jamie asked me with a poised expression on his face. "It would help us both out greatly. Surely you are growing lonely and could use some company."

I wasn't that lonely. It appears they have worked all these details out without me. Sounded familiar, much like what my parents had done. The difference this time was that I had a choice. I wasn't a young girl who saw no other option. I was an adult who had walked away from one marriage of convenience. I had no plans on entering into one again. If I got married again—and that was a big if—it would be because I had fallen in love. And that was an unlikely event since the man I found myself infatuated with wanted nothing to do with me.

"As you can see, we've drawn up the contracts." Corrin handed me a folder.

I accepted the folder only because I'd been curious. My eyes burned from the rage building inside of me. "Could you two give Lord Jamie and me a few minutes?"

My siblings jumped to their feet and scurried off. It was clear they thought everything was going to work out how they hoped, except it wasn't. I took the file with me as I approached the bar to pour myself a good stiff drink. It would require the hard stuff to get through this conversation without losing my shit.

"Drink?" I asked as I poured about four fingers into the glass.

Jamie nodded and grabbed a seat across from me proudly. "So, when do you want to do this?"

I nearly choked on the liquid fire coating my throat. Once I recovered, I chanced another drink and tilted my head up so I could look anywhere but at the man sitting in front of me.

"I'm thinking a spring wedding would be nice. It will give us time to properly introduce me to your family and country. Show them what we have is the real deal..."

I cut him off quickly. "But it's not. There is nothing between us. We haven't even spoken since I left Spain."

His hand gripped the glass tighter, making his knuckles go white. "There was a time you felt differently."

It took all I had not to scream at him. "I was fourteen, Jamie. Fourteen."

"You were fifteen when..."

Again, I stopped him there. "Okay, I was fifteen. You cannot seriously think I even comprehended what the hell I wanted at fifteen. All I understood at that point in my life was that I needed out of the crazy family I'd been living with. The drama of daily life was more than I wished to be a part of. My life now is not the same. Hell, my life a year later was not the same. Do you remember what I said the day I told you I was leaving?"

"You didn't mean it. You were only saying what you thought I needed to hear. I realize that now."

My calm demeanor vanished. *"I meant every fucking word. You may have been my first, but you were not the only boy I'd let fuck me. Why do you think the Prat boys enjoyed hanging out with me that summer?"*

I'd never watched someone turn the color purple before. Ramon would become red-faced with anger, but never purple. I was a little worried about it.

"Don't say that." His unruffled voice did not match his expression. *"Don't say that. Don't lie to me. You will regret it."*

I decided to move the conversation along and leave him to process the fact this would never go anywhere. "I'm not doing this."

Jamie sat there stock-still, wearing a blank expression. His eyes were hallowed and cold, the surrounding room even held a chill to it. I grabbed the folder and walked over to the fireplace. "I think it would be best if you and my siblings left first thing tomorrow." I tossed the papers in the fire and turned to leave.

A hand gripped my forearm before I could make my path to the door. I would have bruises there in the morning. "You will see things my way, Angela. I'll make sure of it. You will eventually be mine like you promised."

I'd never been more appreciative that Edward insisted I learn a little self-defense. He knew his men could not be with me all the time. There were times they would leave me alone and I might find myself in a situation that may require I know at least how to escape out of a hold. Catching him off, I drove my elbow back into him, then used my heel to dig into the top of his foot. That move thankfully encouraged him to release me enough for me to make my exit. My guards were close by and would stop him if he tried to follow. It was another detail I was thankful Edward demanded, assigning a few guards to keep an eye on us.

The next morning, I woke Gabriela and took her for a first

light ride. I wanted to be gone when my guests started moving, so I didn't have to listen as Cora and Corrin attempted to convince me I should reconsider Jamie's offer. By the time we'd returned, two things had occurred. My guests were gone; one I was told had departed last night shortly after I left him in the library. The other was a fire that started in the kitchen. A mysterious flammable substance had been poured on the stove and when the cook turned it on it ignited and spread quickly. The damage was contained to the kitchen, thankfully, and no one was hurt. But the mystery was how it got there. Had someone done it on purpose? Something that had been hard to prove and eventually dismissed as an accident.

We moved back to Aragon, and that is when my relationship with Edward started to redevelop. I glance over to find him sitting silently next to me. He has not said a word since we sat down. The only thing he's done is take his seat and throw an arm around the back of my chair.

"Are you okay?" I ask as I glance to my right where Cora, Corrin, and Jamie are seated.

Edward cracks his neck and clenches his jaw. "Are you going to explain who that tosser is, or are you hoping I'll draw my own conclusions?"

"I told you already, a family friend." I turn my eyes at the stage and shift, doing my best to not get into this here.

"He's not," Edward growls in my ear. "That man has not stopped contemplating my death since I've sat down and placed my claim on you."

That actually makes me chuckle. "Jamie is harmless. He repeatedly requested that I save him from the hairy spiders that would drop onto him in the stable when we were kids. He's always been skittish, and it was my responsibility as one of his only friends to keep him calm."

"What happens when he is not calm?" Edward asks as he places his other hand on my arm.

"I'm not sure. He was always calm around me. Or he was most of the time, at least. I saw a few outbursts, but nothing that ever worried me. There were rumors, though. One boy said he caught him tormenting a dog, but I found that hard to believe. Jamie forever seemed to fear animals, even the gentle horses. A few others declared he had a breakdown when he was seventeen, spent several months in a mental hospital. That happened right after I left Spain, but I don't know if it is true or not."

"Do you believe that rumor?"

I hadn't, but then again, I remember how upset he was when I left. "He was my first. The plan we made when we were just kids was to run off one day and escape from it all. That changed as I got older and we grew apart. Then Ramon came along and before long, I was gone. He took the news hard, so I guess it is possible, but unlikely. His family wouldn't have allowed it; they'd have dealt with it more quietly."

"He's not still mad about that, though, is he? There's more you aren't telling me." I swear the man never gives up when he senses something off.

"About four years ago he showed up to the citadel with those two and a proposal." The lights dim, letting everyone know the opera will start soon. "I dismissed him, and I've not seen or heard from him since."

Edward sits there in silence but his expression alerts me he's working a few details out in his head. He pulls his phone out, and he fires off a text message to someone.

"What was that about?" I ask as the curtain opens.

"Just having the guys look into a few matters. Now, shhh, I've never had the privilege of sitting in the luxury seats while at the opera house. I want to see what all the fuss is about." Edward's hand lands on my leg and my skin under it burns. "One day we are coming to the opera alone so I can have a little fun."

I would have laughed, but before I could a god-awful screeching sound echoes all around us. It's not one you can ignore and has everyone making a fast chaotic exit.

CHAPTER 23
Edward

The Royals

The moment the fire alarm goes off, I know something is wrong. I don't for one second believe this is real. My eyes land on the men I hired, and it seems we are in agreement. The hairs on my neck are tingling, and I realize none of us are prepared for what is going to happen next. My gut clenches because I hate knowing someone has thought this out and is ahead of me.

Angela's hand on my back brings my focus on what I can control. "Do you have your tracker?"

She nods and taps the side of her right breast, then she glances down at her shoes, and tugs on her earrings. My woman is more than prepared, wearing more than one like I taught her to do after an incident in Moscow when her tracker was taken by a guard. Moving forward, she kept the coin in plain sight and wore the toe ring and earrings as a backup.

"You know what to do if something happens. Don't fight them as long as they aren't trying to harm you. Let us do our jobs and trust that no one will permit anything to happen to you." For the very first time in my life, I'm not sure I totally believe what I am telling her.

Gino and Stew step out for a second to determine the best course to get us out of here. We are safe for now. No one can make it past them to get to us. I also know Travis and his men will be here within minutes. Isaac will have sent her team the second he received my text about my suspicions just to be safe. Like me, he'd rather overreact than not react and wish he had.

I study the people in the suite with us to determine how to deal with them. That is when I notice a few things that puts my guard up even more. "Lady Lauren and Lady Robyn, where are your husbands?"

Lauren blushes but tells me. "They never attend the actual opera. They always sneak off to play cards."

"Cards? Here? This is a normal event?" I've not heard of this, and I find that odd.

"It started a few years ago." Robyn sounds irritated. "It is the only way I can even get Saul to join me."

"Who else plays cards with them?" I ask, wondering if maybe this has something to do with that instead of what I fear it might.

They list some very wealthy men. I'm not surprised either. Before I can question them more, Ian Hilton burst through the door and motions for his wife to join him. Lauren and he may seem like an odd pair, but it is clear by the way he embraces her what they have is the real deal.

"Sir Edward, I am going to take these ladies with me if that is okay with you?" His eyes meet mine. "Lord Saul is having our car pulled around."

I nod and watch as her friends follow, Lady Cara included. They understand how this works. Until the coast is clear, until we can assure Angela's safe departure, we will be going nowhere. A mob making a hasty exit adds a risk we don't like.

Several minutes pass. The longer we sit here, the more uneasy I become. When I feel my phone vibrate inside my suit jacket, I go to reach for it.

"It's a shame, really." Lord Jamie states.

"What's a shame?" I ask, curious about why he's decided to speak now.

Taking his seat again, he relaxes as if getting comfortable for a long conversation. "How easy this all was. I expected it to be a challenge, but sadly was disappointed. In only a matter of minutes, this will all be over and I'll finally get what was promised to me years ago."

His eyes land on Angela and the way he admires her makes me want to punch him. I know I could take him easily, so very easily in fact. The only reason I don't is because of his relaxed state. He knows something I don't and I need him to share his knowledge with me before I bust his arse.

Cora and Corrin are deep in conversation, unaware of the odd behavior from their guest. And that bothers me, too. Why am I the only one who sees this man has issues?

"God, you two are annoying?" Lord Jamie shakes his head disgusted. "Would you just stop the yapping and have a seat? The show is about to begin."

Corrin makes an awful face. "I believe the opera..."

"Not that show, Corrin, the one we came to watch. The one that will reveal so much and end with the death of a man ready to give his life for those he's sworn to protect. An honorable way to die. His country will forever remember him for his sacrifice."

I hear Cora gasp and feel Angela stiffen behind me. Her worst fear since we got back together was that I'd lose my life trying to save hers. It is why she ordered me to promise her I won't.

"Jamie, we can work this out," Angela speaks in a shaky voice. "There is no reason for anyone to die."

Hollow, disturbed eyes fall on us. "There is always a reason for someone to die."

Cora makes a run for the door, but Jamie stops her with his words. "Running will only get you shot."

The chair next to her explodes, sending white fiber flying into the air. There was no warning, just an eruption when the bullet penetrated the cushion. It could have easily taken any of us out.

Instinct has me positioning myself on the other side of Angela. Doing a scan of the dark opera house for any signs where the shooter is perched. All I see is darkness and a few shadows. I know the person has to be somewhere directly across from us by the angle the bullet stuck the chair. There is no way for them to remain hidden for long. Soon they will have to reveal themselves if they plan on taking another shot.

Lord Jamie rubs his chin. "The first time I saw someone die, it was as if I came alive. Watching the life drain from a person is a rush. The only other time I ever felt alive was when I was with you. Why did you change our plans, Angela?"

"We were kids, Jamie. Kids who didn't understand how ridiculous it was to assume running away would make everything better. And like most things in your childhood, we grew apart. It wasn't your fault. It wasn't my fault. It just happens." Angela is doing her best to remain calm, but I hear the panic in her voice. "Don't do this. Don't force me to hate you."

Her words snag his attention. "Hate me? No. Did you hate me when those before him died?"

"What are you talking about?" Angela's grip on my arm tightens.

Sounding bored, he explains. I barely believe what I am hearing. It seems this man has been very busy. Her head buries into my back as she cries, realizing she has caused the death of a few good men because this arsehole considered them to be a threat. Found a way to make one death appear natural—heart attack. Then there were the accidents you didn't question—drowning, car accident, and overdosing. My blood goes cold at the thought this psycho has gotten away with the death of four men, one I hadn't even realized died until he mentioned him. I had wanted to end Marcel's life after I learned of his involvement with her, but I would never actually carry through. Lord Jamie did, however, and he did it in a manner that let me appreciate the lengths he was willing to go.

"You know which one I found the most satisfying?" He stares at the ceiling and smiles. "It was when I convinced a woman scorned to take out the man responsible. Telling her what she needed, how to do so, and then waiting for her to do it. I wish I'd been there when it happened as I had been for the others. Watched the life drain from his body with the satisfaction of knowing I got my revenge for him stealing what was mine." A sick laugh explodes out of him. "I fooled you all. I knew then no one could stop me. That I was invincible. Playing with the lives of others was extremely rewarding and better than any drug out there. Plus, it pays well."

"Why?" Angela squeaks out once she catches her breath. "You were always so gentle and kind. Made me kill the spiders in the barn because..."

He shrugs and sneers. "The act of killing always bothered me. But watching it was thrilling, is still thrilling. It is why I hire someone to do the killing while I sit back and enjoy the show. Come and sit with me, Angela. I'll show you what I mean. We can watch it together this time. And when it is done, we can get out of here and live the life you promised me. Come on. The show is about to begin. You will be safer over here by me. Sir Edward is about to become what every guard dreams of when he pledges his life to protect the throne. It will be my best work to date and one I will remember forever."

I had no way of showing her what I already knew without moving her from behind my back. While Lord Jamie was sharing all he has been up to, Isaac and the rest of the King's Guards have been busy listening. Searching the opera house for the person who took the shot earlier. Gino and Stew are in position again, ready to do what needs to be done to protect Angela if it comes to that. They were now inside the suite, willing to act on a moment's notice.

My phone has been vibrating, pulsing under my jacket in code for the last several minutes. I understood the morse code being repeated against my chest was what the plan was and when it would transpire. The countdown was ticking. The shooter has been located and apprehended quietly. The show that would soon occur was not the one he was expecting. It would be the end game for him, and I don't even feel bad about that after hearing his confession. This man does not deserve to live another day. He's lived too many as it is and the world will be better off with him gone.

"It's too bad you know." Lord Jamie starts talking again. "You choosing a dead man over me. I guess she was right. She said I was a fool for loving you instead of her. She warned me you'd rather die with him than have a life with me." He glances across the room and does a rolling motion with his hand before he aims his eyes on us.

It's time. I do not want her to see this. I twist and wrap her in my arms, securing her against my chest as I take us both to the ground in one rapid movement. Covering her body with mine just in case something goes amiss. The high-pitched scream of Cora notifies me the moment it comes together. The feel of a large hand on my back directs me I can move. I stand with her still close to my chest and get the fuck out of there.

As soon as we are in the hallway, I can breathe again. My feet keep moving and so do hers. She is trembling so violently I'm a little concerned. I'm certain it is the adrenaline rush, but there is no way I'm taking any chances. When we reach the SUV waiting to drive us away from this hell, I scoop her up and settle her inside with me. Order the driver to take us to the hospital.

"I'm fine," Angela whispers into my chest. "Just take me home, please."

I kiss the top of her head and do as she has requested. I'll call the doctor if she doesn't calm soon, have them give her a sedative if need be.

"What the fuck just happened?" she asks after we've been driving for a while. "And who the hell is she?"

I have been asking myself that same question. I'm not sure we will ever figure it out now that Jamie is gone. But I will dig through his life and contacts until I'm satisfied Angela is safe. I'll not rest until every last stone and name has been investigated and dismissed. No one will ever threaten her like this again.

CHAPTER 24
Angela

The Royals

The last five days have been a nightmare. I did not know Jamie had been so engrossed in the details of my life all these years. From what Edward could figure out, the man had perfected how to be a chameleon. Very proficient at hiding in plain sight and blending in. It was scary to realize how many times he'd been within arm's reach of me.

Isaac has been proving he was an excellent replacement for Edward. It only took him hours to locate a flat Jamie owned in a shady neighborhood. His headquarters, where he not only ran his underground assassin business, but where he sat and waited and watched me all too closely.

It was hard for me to picture the young boy I once knew as a killer. The shy kid who was afraid of his own shadow. The one who didn't speak unless he had something imperative to say. The kid who remained quiet and always seemed to be taking it all in.

Watching. It seems like the older he got, the more he enjoyed the watching part. Me. Those he believed were interfering. Men. Women. Edward.

When I closed my eyes, his voice in my head grew louder.

His confession of killing the first man I'd had an affair with after Ramon, did something to me. I remember how I felt when I learned the man had died a few months after I broke it off. Thought it odd that a healthy male suffered a heart attack, but it happens. Then to be made aware that three other men lost their lives for daring to touch me. The last one being Marcel, who had been found only days ago in a brothel just outside of Beijing. They ruled his death as an overdose, but if Jamie spoke the truth, it was murder and he had been there to watch it all go down.

I wasn't sure if I accepted his confession of Ramon's death. I guess it is possible he befriended Sofia and planted the idea in her head. But planting an idea was not the same as carrying out the act. I'm not so sure she hadn't already been considering it. The fact she confessed and never once mentioned someone else assisted her rubbed me wrong. Jamie, in my mind, wanted to believe he'd been a part of it because of his hatred for everything that was my life.

"You have to stop." Edward plops down by my feet on the lounge where I'm seated. "What he did is not your fault."

"It feels like it is." I shiver even though I am sitting in front of the fireplace wrapped in a throw. "These men died because of me. *You* almost died because of me."

He stands, and that is when I notice how he is dressed. A man should not look so fine wearing dark sweat pants and a tank top. "What's the point of wearing sweats and a tank? They seem like an odd combination."

Taking the folder from my hands, he closes it and drops it on the floor. Then he reaches for my hand and tugs. "Up."

I'm wearing frumpy clothes. Larkin bought me a few nice pairs of fuzzy pajamas for Christmas, and I never realized how comfy they were until now. I have lounged around in them for a few days. I don't want to move, but I do.

I stare at his arse while he drags me behind him. "Did you know that those fit you nicely?"

Edward shakes his head. "My sweats?"

"Yes. Are you wearing underwear?" I reach up and tug on the waistband to discover he is not. "Why do you hate them so much?"

Now he is laughing at me. "Underwear?"

"Yes. I mean, I understand when you are relaxing how that might be freeing. I forgo the bra when I can to let the girls breathe."

He reaches the door that leads to the backyard. The area I've avoided since the day that picture was delivered to my phone. The one I was looking at when Edward sent it skidding across the floor. "Why do you care? I just find them restricting, okay?"

"Do you wear them when you work out? It seems like it would get uncomfortable letting everything bounce around down there." I glance down because I can. I am rewarded with the outline of what he carries between his legs. I want to drop to my knees and worship him the way he often does me.

"Don't even think about it. Strip." I do a quick perusal of the area. "I sent everyone away. It is just us."

"Why are we here?" I point at the door and what I know is behind it. "I'm not comfortable going out there naked."

He squints his eyes, reaches behind him, and yanks his tank right over his head. After he's tossed it on the floor, he slips his thumbs into his waistband and shoves the sweats down his legs, then steps out of them. "Suit yourself. I'm going to enjoy the heated mineral pool you own. Give my muscles a chance to experience the soothing only it can provide. I thought it would be nice to enjoy it together, but if you aren't going to join me, I'll do it alone."

I cannot believe he is about to step outside in the buff for anyone to see him. "Someone might see you."

Edward shrugs and grabs his dick, which is rapidly growing. "So, they see me."

"That's a huge violation of your privacy." I hug my arms and shiver again. I've been so cold lately.

"Only if I let it be. I mean, yes, it is, but if I let what happened to you out there dictate me never enjoying that pool, then I've allowed the person responsible to win. Is that how you wish to live, *Anjo*. Or do you prefer to be given a choice?" He extends his hand and waits. "I'd like to help you win back what you lost. Prove that you are in control again. Take back what someone tried to steal from you."

"I don't think I can." I close my eyes as tears stream down my face. It kills me to be so helpless, but that is how I feel right now.

Edward's hands land on my face and I hate I am disappointing him. "You can, but only you can decide when that will be." He leans in and kisses my lips softly before he opens the door and struts out to the pool without a care in the world.

I know it's cold out there. That the pool is heated and warm. I watch as he stretches his arms wide and swings them as he spins in a circle, giving anyone who could be watching a show. He pounds his chest hard and lets out a roar that sounds more like a battle cry. When he is done, he turns to face me, winks, and falls backward into the water with a carefree attitude and not at all concerned.

I watch him float on his back for several minutes before I decide he's right. If I want to move past all this, then it is up to me to do so. He can't do it for me, even though he'd love to. It has to be my choice and mine alone.

Fuck this shit. Fuck everyone and everything. Fuck all those who dared to make me feel like I had to hide and be a certain way. This is my life. This is my home. It's the only one I am ever going to live, and I'm going to own it and enjoy it. I am done letting others make me feel like I can't be the person I've always been on the inside. The woman who was brave enough to walk out on a man who cared for no one. I will no longer pretend to be someone I am not. I will proudly let my colors fly and hold my head high.

I disrobe in the hall and grab the handle. Taking in a deep breath, I open the door and shriek as the cold bitter air hits my skin. Before I chicken out, I jog for the pool. I almost laugh out loud when I decide it is time for some fun and do what I would have done when I was younger.

In a voice so loud it echoes off the walls, I yell, "Cannonball!" then leap into the air and make the biggest splash I can. My arse grazes the bottom of the pool before I float to the top. As soon as I emerge, I'm engulfed in powerful arms and pulled against his bare chest. His dick is hard against my back as his lips land on my neck.

"Hi," I laugh.

"Hi," he growls.

"I want to do that again," I tell him as I squirm free and swim for the steps. I climb out and shiver. "Fuck, it's cold."

Edward is right behind me and the warmth of his body helps. "Are we yelling again or just jumping?"

I love this man. He gets me more than anyone else ever did. "Yelling, of course. You can't do a cannonball without yelling it."

"Point well made." He takes a bow and gives me a wink.

He takes off and yells right as he leaps into the air and splashes me. I am right behind him doing my damndest to enjoy myself. We do that for about ten minutes before I decide I've had my fill of the cold air. I swim up to him and wrap my body around his.

"Better?" His smile is sexy as fuck.

"Yes." I lean forward and kiss his lips. "Thank you."

"I didn't do anything, not really." His hands squeeze my arse. "I love you, *Anjo*. I only want to see you this happy always."

His eyes say he isn't lying. I could get so absorbed in them, have gotten lost in them. It is then I know that my life will not be complete without him. I take my hands and run them through his reddish-brown curls, down his beautiful face, across his soft lips, and over his rough beard. I never thought I'd want this again, that I'd consider doing this, but I do, and I know it will be up to me to do the asking.

"Edward, my love." God, I'm so nervous. "I love you. Want you in my life. Never wish to spend another day without you by my side. I want us to be more than significant others, lovers, or even best friends who love to fuck the other person into utopia. I would prefer to be allowed to introduce you as my husband. To change my last name to match yours. Will you marry me?"

He blinks several times, completely shocked by my words. But the smile that spreads over his face gives me the answer before he is able to get his mouth and brain to say them. "Fuck yes. When? Where?"

I shrug. "I've not thought that far ahead."

My body is shifted back until the head of his dick is lined up with my opening. "I'm going to fuck you out here. It will be a celebration fuck that is sure to give those guarding us an earful. Then I'm taking you inside and carrying you to our room, fucking you again for blowing my mind and making me a very happy man. Once we've recovered from that one, we'll talk about the details and decide when and where. I love you." Edward slams me down on him, and I swear I come so fast and hard, if he weren't holding me, I'd drown.

He fucks me like only he can. Brings me to heights I've only ever reached with him. Has me begging him to give me more until he is unable to hold back his own orgasm. Then he lets go and the roar that falls from his lips echoes around us.

On wobbly legs, he carries me, wet and naked, to our bedroom and drops us on the bed. We are a mess, but we don't care. All we care about is taking our time and showing each other how much we appreciate each other. It is a wonder either of us can move once we are done.

Clothed in robes, Edward leads me down to the kitchen to

rehydrate and put some much-needed carbs in our tired bodies. He tosses a pile of blankets and pillows on the floor in front of the still roaring fireplace. Tugs me down next to him and starts to feed me.

"I have something for you." Edward leans back.

"Again," I tease. "I thought a man in his fifties needed time to recover."

His green eyes are filled with sparks of fire, and I know I'm likely to pay for that later. "I meant I possess something I've been holding onto and now I want you to have it."

I was about to smart off again, but the box he has in his hand stops me. "When did you get that?"

He opens it and pulls out a ring. "It was my mother's."

"Your mother's?" It's gorgeous.

"Yep. My father saved and saved and saved to buy this for her. She never took it off. When she died, my sister put it in a safe and kept it. Her husband bought her a lovely ring, and she didn't see the point of replacing it, but thought I'd want it one day. When Gerald died, she still didn't want it, even though I told her I would never need it. I got it from her on Christmas, so I'd have it to give to you when the time was right." He grabs my hand and slides it on my left finger. "I know it's not..."

"It's perfect," I tell him. "Perfect."

CHAPTER 25
Edward

The Royals

S itting on my arse doing nothing isn't working for me. I am
bored out of my fucking mind. Since I was a young man,
I've worked. Not just worked but been part of a team that
had problems to solve, issues to deal with, situations that required
planning, and a lot of investigating so you never got caught with
your pants down. There was always something that needed my
attention, and now there isn't.

While I love the life Angela and I are living, fucking her into a
trance, waking next to me, spending time with her just being us,
it's not enough. She still has a job that requires her to put in long
hours daily. Me hovering in her office at home or the palace is only
annoying both of us.

Which is why, after I dropped her off today, I decided it was
time to figure out what I was going to do. Working was a must for
a man like me, downtime will only get me into trouble. I've
thought about this the last few days. I employ a great deal of skills
that can be put to use in a number of private sectors. But a job in
security is not high on my list. I want something different, a

position more challenging. It is why I am walking into this office with a plan of attack.

The officer seated at the main desk glances up, a little unsure. "Can I help you, Sir Edward?"

When you have been the Captain of the King's Guards for as many years as I have, those in certain branches recognize you. Most of the time when I've visited this branch, it was because we had a problem that required I speak with someone who knew Aragon better than I did. I spent hours here after Princess Violet returned, gathering as much intel about Ruben and his organization as I could. It wasn't my responsibility to police the city. My task was only to protect and serve the Royal Family. That often required me to reach out to others whose role was about the people living in Hermosa Islas.

"Is Chief Investigator Hawkins available?" I know he is expecting me, but it's possible he got pulled away doing his job.

After a quick check, I am told to head back to his office. I know the officer is curious about why I'm here. For now, I am only here to talk. Nothing has been decided, just me putting a few feelers out there to determine if maybe I'd be welcome.

"Sir Edward, to what do I owe the honor?" CI Vance Hawkins stands and greets me with a handshake.

"Can't I just stop by and chat with a friend?" I take my seat and notice the stack of folders on his desk. "You look like you have your hands full there."

"You cannot possible realize how true that is. Finding good dependable help these days..." He pauses mid-sentence and I can see the wheels in his head spinning faster. "You're bored."

"Why do you say that?" I shift uncomfortably in my chair.

"Because you are looking at my stack of folders the way a man looks at a stripper after a long dry spell." Hawkins leans back in his chair and laughs. "Fuck me sideways."

"I'd rather not." I scratch my head. "You painted a very interesting image there, by the way."

"So you really aren't going back? You actually retired." He shakes his in disbelief.

"I really retired. Conflict of interest." I don't elaborate.

"I never thought I'd see the day you would let..."

"Be very careful what you say next. Angela and I are getting married. It would be inappropriate for the Captain of the Guards to be married to a member of the Royal Family." I didn't want to feel the need to punch the man for saying something disrespectful. He's known to repeat things that are not polite to keep matters light. If it were anyone other than Angela, I'd not have cared, but she is more than a joke or a fuck. She is the woman I love, and I'll not let anyone degrade her, even if it is done in fun. "Now, tell me why there is a stack of files on your desk. Don't you have a team of investigators to do the grunt work for you?"

The frown that takes over his face lets me know I just asked the right question. "We had a big shake up a few weeks ago. I lost a handful of my men to some shady practices I hadn't been aware of. Now, I'm shorthanded with a bunch of green investigators who aren't ready for a case as important as this one. Until I hire someone who doesn't get squeamish at a crime scene, I'll be doing my job and this one."

"That bad?" I point at the files. "Or is it you don't think they have the balls to handle a case like that?"

"Both." Hawkins sits up and rests his arms on the desk. "Why are you here? Please tell me it's because you want a job. One that will keep you up late, make you scratch your head, and require you to go home later and fuck until you can't think."

"I have a few requirements that you may not want to hear or be willing to accept." I list them and watch him nod his head. While I prefer to work, I also need to be able to travel when my lady does. No way am I letting her be gone for weeks at a time with me not around to take care of her.

I barely finish before he asks, "When can you start?"

"You're that desperate, are you?" I chuckle. "Give me a couple of weeks. I've got a few matters that need settled first. I didn't exactly expect to land a job today."

"Then why the fuck did you come to me? Fine. Two weeks and not a day longer." He grabs a box off his floor, empties it, and then drops the folders from his desks into it. "Take this shit with you. Look it over in your spare time. That shit is now yours. Maybe you can figure out who has picked up where the Del Markov's left off. I never thought I'd say this, but I'll take those immoral bastards back if only to get this new one gone. He's making Viktor look like a pussycat, and if we don't shut this arsehole down soon, King Antonio is going to start cracking heads. I'm making that your problem since you have a rapport with him."

"How come I'm just hearing about this?" I can't believe this is new news.

"Remember why I told you I was short staffed? Yeah, now you understand what I was referring to." He leans back again in his chair. "Are you sure the lady will be okay with you working for the NPB? We don't pay nearly as good as the King's Guards."

"The lady will be fine with it. I'm not doing this for the money." I'm not completely sure she'll love that I'm diving into a job that puts me in a different kind of danger. I am, however, confident she will support me and my decision.

"Now get the fuck out of here. I've got work to do and you are keeping me from it." He motions to the door. "Call me if you have any questions."

I grab the box. "Thanks, Vance, I appreciate this."

"Remember that when you're buried arse deep in paperwork and cussing me out because that box is the devil's work."

I shouldn't be smiling about having to go through a box of shit, but fucking hell I am. I'm ready to get my hands into a task that will make me feel like I'm doing something useful. Once I grab some lunch, I'm taking over Angela's home office and getting to work.

CHAPTER 26
Edward

The Royals

The Constitutional Ball is an annual event that takes place every January to celebrate the year we adopted our current constitution. Only those of importance are ever invited, which means it's a stuffy, snobby bunch. The only thing that makes it tolerable is the fact I get to admire my lady, who is dressed to kill.

I swear when she picked her gown for tonight's ball, it was done so to drive me crazy. The low-cut back rests just above the bumblebee tattoo I know well. The same one I licked right before she sent me away to get ready. It's tight in all the best places, squeezes her bosoms in that way that has them spilling out of the top, and hugs her ass and legs, making me hard. There will be no fucking in the private hallway tonight without ruining her gown. I'll have to wait until we return home to peel it off of her and then punish her for teasing me all night.

Since the King and his brothers are all now married, a few other details surrounding the celebration have changed. The afterparty no longer is an event. Princess Gabriela didn't throw much of a fuss about it. Her priorities have shifted to bigger issues;

she doesn't have time to party. And Princess Isabel is still too young for a party of that caliber.

Plus, now that they have children, those who are old enough to handle this celebration are allowed to attend. Brigham and Juliet, Violet's siblings, are also in attendance tonight. Charlotte stayed through dinner before she got bored and wanted to join her siblings and cousins upstairs. Having the children helped make the banquet more entertaining. Getting to watch the Reyes clan interact as one big happy family showed everyone how close they were. I admired how the boys I once supervised have grown into men determined to set an example and be better than those who came before them.

We are now in the socializing part of the evening and I seriously am ready to leave. This is not me. I'm not a man who can pretend to be okay with the judgments this group of socialites believes they have the right to bestow on us. I've heard more than once how kind it was of Angela to allow me to escort her tonight. Overheard them whispering about how it was a shame that the Royal Family seems to have fallen into a pattern and taken pity on the less fortunate.

I've walked amongst this crowd and had to keep tight lips while I stood by her side and listened to them blow wind. My brandy consumption is probably going to make my liver revolt for a week. It's been a long time since I've felt the effects the way I am and it may explain my next move.

As soon as the current snobbish couple decides they have said all they wish to say, I grab her hand and begin dragging her behind me.

"Where are we going?" My lovely fiancée questions with an amused tone.

"They've taken up enough of your time. I'm tired of listening to them and their blah blah blah," I grumble. "Fucking judgmental ungracious bunch of twat waffles. If I have to listen to one more of them tell you congratulations with that expression of pity, things could turn ugly."

"You can't let them get to you, Edward. They are only jealous that I found something they have not." She surprises me by patting my arse for all to see. "Not to mention I've done what some of them were not able to do."

We reach the dance floor, and I waste no time sweeping her into my arms and leading her around. It's been years since I've danced with a woman. My wife loved to dance, and she taught me well. I stopped dancing after her death. Holding Angela securely in my arms reminds me why I once loved pirouetting and why I plan on keeping her out here for as long as I can.

After a few spins around the floor, I slow it down. "What have you done they could not?

Angela glances up at me with adoring eyes. She takes her left hand, where my ring proudly rests on her finger, and runs it through my hair and down the back of my neck. Then she leaves it there as she drags me closer. "Captured your attention longer than for only one night."

I growl again and feel the blood in my body rush to my cock. "You had my attention long before, my love. They were only..."

Her other hand lands on my lips. "I know. They don't appreciate it, though. You were the trophy so many of them were hoping to enjoy. Now I've taken you out of the game they prefer to play, and several of them dislike that."

I grab her wrist to remove her hand as I lean forward. "I fucking love you."

As soon as the words are out of my mouth, my lips fall on hers. I know we are drawing attention, but I don't give a damn. Let them watch me claim my woman who has agreed to be mine forever. I want them all to understand I'm in this for the long haul, hers for the keeping. I need them to witness the difference between what I was like when I gave in to temptation, and how I am with the woman who owns me.

When I release her, she blinks a few times, dazed. "Wow."

We dance until I know she needs a break. I lead her to the bar to get us both some water and let her take a seat. I'm sure her feet must be killing her in the shoes she slipped them into tonight. Four-inch heels are not intended to be worn for hours of dance and socializing. They are ornamental and require the woman to sit and rest.

Her friends join us, and I must admit I like them. Their presence brings a calmness that permits her to relax. I stand and give up my seat so Lady Cara can sit. It is then I notice only one of them has an escort.

"Where is Lord Saul? Is there a card game you forgot to tell me about going on behind closed doors?" I try to make a joke but see it is not taken well. "I'm sorry I was only..."

Lady Robyn sets her drink down. "It's fine. He is on a *business* trip." The tone she carries as she spits out business has me doubting that. "He hates these events anyway, so it is best this way."

Lady Lauren grabs Angela's hand and sighs as she stares at the ring I placed there. "I know I've seen this a hundred times, but each time it hits me right here."

"You are causing quite a stir tonight, Sir Edward," Lady Cara snickers. "So many pouting faces ready to take your woman down for stealing you away from them."

"She did no such thing." I roll my eyes, irritated. "I have always been hers for the taking."

"I know that. Lauren knows that. Robyn figured it out when you came stomping in, when that other bloke was intruding. But if you think for one second they care, then you, sir, have been living under a rock. As far as this group of brooding tarts are concerned, she trampled in where she was not allowed to trample.

Now they want her head, figuratively, of course." She swirls her drink and points it at one particular female. "With her being the exception. That woman has not been the same since you bedded her. She, I believe, may actually take both of yours if she gets the chance."

Lady Catherine holds my gaze for a moment before she whirls to walk away. If looks could kill, the lot of us would be deceased.

"One night. Not that good of a night, either," I admit, and all five of them laugh, Ian included. "Know what I mean, man?"

He chuckles a little louder. "I do. I mean, I've never uhm..."

When he stumbles with his words, I help him. "Fucked her?"

He blushes and glances at his wife, embarrassed. "Yes, that. But I have had a few not so enjoyable encounters with others like her."

I elbow him. "You can say it, Ian. Report it for all to hear. You've had a few unsatisfactory fucks in your days. Because fucking is often just that, and not all of them are worth going back for seconds or thirds. One fuck is all you dare to suffer through."

His wife is trying not to laugh at her husband's uneasiness with my bluntness. "Sure. I'll agree to that. Once is more than enough sometimes."

My hand grips his shoulder. "And then you find the one that is worth all the fucks you've got left and more."

"Edward!" Angela chastises me for being so frank. "You are embarrassing him."

"Am I? Nah, he gets it. Why do you think he married your friend? Do you expect it was because he fucked her once and said *not bad*? Nope. It was because it became more than that, was more than that likely to begin with. Love, my dear, makes it so much more. No matter how many times you have her, it is not enough. Am I right, Ian? Tell them I'm right." I give his shoulder a good solid squeeze again for encouragement.

His eyes land on Lauren and the smile that takes over his face has her melting. "He's right. Do you want to take another spin around the dance floor before we go?"

Lauren nods and finishes her drink. "I'd love to. Ladies, have a lovely evening."

Angela takes my hand as she shares. "You know he never says two words around us."

"He's intimidated by you ladies. I'll get him to open up. I bet he's a lot of fun." I lean forward and kiss her cheek. "I need to take a piss. Finish up so we can join them."

She stands "I could use the loo, as well. Why don't you walk me there and when we're done you can take me home? I'm done if you are."

I walk her to the women's lavatory before heading to the men's across the room. She didn't want to use the private one typically designated for the family, said it was too much of a bother. This crowd is one that can often be trusted, so I gave it no thought.

Until I hear several females screaming. They are quickly followed by the sound of pounding feet running past me. Now my heart is in my chest and I cannot move fast enough.

CHAPTER 27
Angela

The Royals

E dward has clearly had a few too many. It is time to take
him home so he can relax and forget about this
judgmental bunch of tossers. I was tiring of it as well.
Done with smiling and pretending for them. I am bored with it
all. The way they think they can say whatever they want. How
they hold my family to higher standards than they themselves live
by. I'm done playing their game and ready to move past it.

When I enter the lavatory, I am alone. I know I should have
probably used the one designated for the family, but I am feeling
rebellious. I do what I need to do and start to wash my hands.

Lady Catherine steps up next to me and waves her hand under
the faucet. There has always been tension between us. I'm not sure
why, really. We went to boarding school together and she never
once was friendly to me. I guess she had plans I interfered with like
so many others did. I will not apologize for any of it. Her
bitterness now has to do with Edward. Again, I'll not apologize,
because she had her chance with him, and he is the one who
passed her over, not me.

"Did he give you that?" She is glaring down at my left hand.

I smile when I gaze down at the jewelry proudly displayed there. "It was his mother's ring."

"How lovely." The sarcasm in her voice cannot be mistaken.

I don't respond. I finish and exit with her not far behind. When we step into the corridor, I try not to make it seem as if I am moving faster, but getting away from her would make me feel better. Something about her makes me uncomfortable, I can sense the air shifting around me.

The moment we walk into the Throne Room is when the chaos starts. One of the large chandelier's bulbs all burst at once, sending sparks falling and causing several female guests to scream. It sends the crowd into a panic. They swarm and quickly move for the exits, compelling me to go with them, even though I don't necessarily want to. Another group of bulbs burst, encouraging them to move faster, making it difficult to stay upright. I know better than to stop or I'll get trampled, so I allow the crowd to push me along and do my best to remain calm. As soon as we are outside, I can step aside and find my way to one of the guards.

Before we reach the door, a sharp object is pressed into my side. I recognize then that none of this was an accident. A hand grasps my elbow and holds me inside with the mob. I have no choice but to stay the course, no one will hear my cries over the others. I continue to shuffle my feet while I do my best to think of how I am going to get away from the person pressing a blade to my side.

"Keep moving." A voice whispers from behind me. "Unless you want to bleed out here for all to see, you will do as you are told and not draw unwanted attention."

Edward's words come to the forefront of my mind, the ones he always repeated about not fighting a capture unless it was a matter of life and death. To trust those who were sworn to protect me and let them do what they did best. So that is what I do. I keep my feet moving and pray that in all the chaos surrounding us, someone will notice I'm not where I am supposed to be.

"Now turn right." I know that voice, recognize it.

"They will be looking for me soon," I warn the person forcing me away from the mob into the darkness.

"And when they find you, it will be too late. Tell me, sister, why do you always insist on stealing what was meant to be mine?"

My feet stumble as realization washes over me. All this time it was Cora.

"First, it was father. Then, it was the kids at school. When I had a chance to get away, you stole that too." She sounds so bitter and cold. "You weren't even able to appreciate the life you took from me. You never valued any of it like I would have. Never deserved to have the privileges you were just granted all because of a title you never respected."

"Cora, what are you talking about? I held everything seriously. It was Ramon who..."

"Shut up! Our brother even found you more valuable than me, because of it. I was the one who made sure he always got what he wanted, but he could never see past all the privileges they granted you." The blade presses against me a little harder. "I would have been a better Queen had I been given the chance."

"It is not all it is cracked up to be, Cora," I tell her honestly.

I don't think she hears me, though, because she keeps rambling, not making any sense. "And when you turned Lord Jamie down on his stupid proposal that I told them both would never work, I thought it was my turn to show him he was focused on the wrong sister. But no, he assumed he could change your mind and cause you to see that you always belonged to him.

"His obsession gave me an idea. It made it easy to get under your skin, play with your mind, and make you feel how I felt most of my life. I told him to take Sir Edward out, that he would get in the way. But no one ever listens to me. They will listen now, though. Once you are gone, they will have no choice but to listen."

It is clear she is no longer in touch with reality. I'm not sure how I never put two and two together. But it all is starting to piece together in my mind. "You sent me the photo of me in my pool?"

She cackles, and it sends tremors down my spine. "I took it the last time I visited you. You went for a midnight swim to relax. I sat in the dark and watched. Snapped a few photos without anyone thinking anything of it."

"The ones of me and Edward in the meadow?" I ask, trying to recall if she was around. I know she was around a lot back then, so it is possible I just don't remember.

"That was Jamie," she informs me, sounding disgusted. "He'd been stalking you for years by then. Keeping close watch to see who he needed to destroy next. But Edward was not a man he thought he could so easily get to, so he let him live like a fool. I stole it from him when he was too afraid to act. Sent it to ensure he was the one they suspected was tormenting you.

"Jamie's biggest fault was that he watched but never acted. It wasn't his style to reach out and let you see he was watching. But what was the point in it all if you didn't appreciate his effort? So, I helped him by going behind his back and sending you all those little gifts. It seemed like the right thing to do at the time. He was very upset with me when he found out what I had done."

"The opera? Did you know of his plan?" I remember how shaken up she had been, but was that only an act? Was she as equally disturbed as him?

"Corrin invited him to the opera. I didn't even realize he was joining us. So, my reaction to it all was very real." Cora stops moving and I realize this is my chance to catch her off guard.

I throw an elbow into her and start to make a run for it, however my heels are not designed for running. The click of a gun cocking stops me dead in my tracks. I spin to find her holding a pistol haphazardly, waving it around, making it even more dangerous now that it is loaded.

"Cora, you should be careful with that. You don't want it to misfire," I warn her.

"Don't tell me what to do." She waves it wildly several more times. And like I warned, it goes off, hits the ground next to my foot, and makes her jump. "Shit."

I want to scream at her for being a fool, but don't. If I yell, I am afraid she will only react in an even more reckless way, so I struggle to remain calm and come up with a plan.

"Well, that was close." She giggles, and it sounds so daunting. "Now don't move, so I can try that again. This is not as easy as it may look."

If she thinks I am going to stand here and let her shoot me, she is crazier than she is acting right now. I will not make this easy on her. Instead, I begin to drift from side to side while I take a step back each time. Getting further into the darkness and away from her, making it harder for her to hit me should she attempt to fire that gun again.

I nearly scream for other reasons, when out of nowhere my arm is snagged, and I'm yanked into the blackness even further. My heart is pounding so hard in my chest I can hear the blood throbbing in my ears.

"Fuck. Angela, stop. This is not how this game is played," Cora shouts when she loses sight of me.

I'm jerked behind a pillar and that is when I become even more confused. "Lady Catherine, what are you doing here?"

"Saving your arse, it seems." She stays low and motions for me to follow her. "Who would have suspected I'd be the one risking my life to save yours."

"Not me." I kick off my heels and begin shadowing her. "Why?"

"Hell, if I know." She pauses and then gestures for me to move again. "Guess I want my chance to take you down myself." Catherine must sense my hesitation because she quickly responds. "I'm kidding. Geez."

As soon as we reach an opening, we make a run for it. I hear Cora cursing and then feel her making chase. It is not easy running in a gown like the one I am wearing. It is extremely restrictive and makes my movements less effective.

The second we round the corner I spot Edward searching frantically and run with all my might toward him. The moment he sees me, he sprints for us.

The sound of a bullet zinging by my head has me ducking. It sends him to the ground as well. The frightened expression in his eyes nearly kills me. I realize this is a scene he's dreaded since he learned I had a stalker and kept it quiet. His fear was that the person after me would take me and he'd not see it, not be able to protect me. Seems he may have been right about that.

"There you are," Cora announces as she approaches from behind. "This is not how I planned your death. Shame on you, Angela. Now I have to kill you in front of them. I wanted to watch them search for you and worry. You ruin everything."

Edward has this alarmed expression in his eyes, knowing what he is about to witness. There will be no way for him to stop it from his position on the ground. So I don't take my eyes off his. I can't. If I am going to die, I want his face to be the last thing I see before I leave this world.

I nearly lose my breath when Gabriela steps out of the crowd. It is not only for the fact I don't want her to see this or get hurt, it is that she has a pistol in her hand. And it is aimed at the person behind me.

"Don't make me do it, Cora," my daughter warns with a voice that expresses to all listening she will shoot.

I'm not sure how long they stand there like that. The world

seems to stop. And when it starts up again, it does so in fast forward.

The sound of a gun firing has my eyes closing as I anticipate getting shot. I hear movement all around me and my daughter muttering a string of curse words as she passes by. Then I am scooped off the ground and against a hard, solid chest. One that I know better than any other and have to wonder if this is real or a dream.

"Fuck. I just lost ten years of my life. Are you okay?" Edward's voice is broken.

"I think so." I take in a deep breath to fill my burning lungs. "Cora was the stalker."

"Fuck," he mumbles into my hair. "Fuck. Fuck. Fuck."

I hold onto him tightly and nuzzle my face deeper into him. "That pretty much sums it up."

Gabriela appears next to me. "Are you okay?"

I reach for her hand and squeeze. "I am. You want to explain that to me?"

"Not now, but I promise I will." She leans in and rests her head against my shoulder. "Damn. Let's not do that again, okay?"

CHAPTER 28
Edward

The Royals

When you watch someone you love nearly die, it changes you. That night will forever be engraved in my brain. I will never forget the fear in Angela's eyes. I will never forget what it felt like when the bullet missed her by only the grace of God. It will be the day that constantly reminds me of the importance of living each day to its fullest and taking nothing or anyone for granted.

Cora was only wounded by the shot that knocked her on her arse. I know Gabriela could have easily put one between her eyes but made a choice to show mercy. It wasn't as if the other woman would get the chance to see the light of day again. She'd be put in a facility that kept her medicated and locked up for the remainder of her life.

After a thorough evaluation, Corrin stopped fighting to get his sister free and walked away. I doubt we will see or hear from him again. He has mixed feelings about the entire situation and it is probably best this way. Sometimes cutting ties allows you the freedom to move on without guilt or remorse.

Cora had been a very busy woman. It all started long ago when they were young. The day Angela stepped into her life, stealing away her father's full attention, something in her brain snapped. The older she got, the more disturbed she became. And when she found out Lord Jamie was obsessed with her sister, she fed his obsession. Helped a man she knew was dangerous to help her ruin Angela's life. Two psychopaths working in tandem to take down someone because she was living her life how she wanted. One of them believed the life Angela had should have been hers. The other felt he'd been tossed aside and never got over it.

The trial to lock Cora up was swift and unyielding. She would spend her days on the third island of Hermosa Islas, the one where all prisoners were sent. It was a secluded landmass, far enough away to keep anyone from escaping. Well guarded by a military base that shared the space. In my mind, they were being too kind letting her live. If I'd have taken the shot that night, she'd not have been given the chance.

Five months have passed and I am finally getting to do what I wanted to do the week after it all went down. I was patient, though, and let Angela handle this family matter first before I made demands.

It's hard to give a woman like Angela something she has never had before. She's traveled the world multiple times over. Owned the finest things. Wore the best designers' clothes. Lived a life full of adventure.

But I could offer her this. A simple wedding. One that involved only those we cared about, family, and a few good friends. On the hilltop where it all started almost fourteen years ago now.

I'd never seen her look more beautiful than she does right now. We aren't dressed in the traditional wedding attire. We are in our everyday clothing, staring into the eyes of the other while we pledge our love to each other. Her son, my King, is overseeing it. Gabriela is standing by her side. My nephew is by mine. The rest of them are behind us in the field, watching. The little ones are running around because they can out here.

When I get the chance to kiss her, I do, and cheers follow. Once it is over, we celebrate with food and laughs and time with our family. Then I whisk her away for a honeymoon she will hopefully enjoy. We could go anywhere, but I wanted her to myself where no one else would be around to bother us.

"A boat?" Angela smiles as she speaks through the headset.

"A yacht I believe is the proper name." I grab her hand. "It will give us privacy."

I explain the plan. Take the boat south and along the coast of Europe, stopping along the way if we choose to do so. We have a month to explore and do whatever it is we want to do. "Do you like that plan, Mrs. Perez?"

"I do, Your Grace." She smiles, knowing I detest my new title. "The Duke of Perez. My very own Duke who was once a Knight."

"You know I hate that I now possess a title," I growl as we make our way to the stateroom.

"But your King insisted on it." She laughs.

I grab her by the waist and toss her over my shoulder. "Against my wishes. But it seems my wife, Her Royal Highness, went behind my back and agreed to such a crazy practice."

"Your wife has a new title as well." She informs me as I toss her on the bed.

"Yes, she does. Mrs.," I inform her as I kiss her lips.

"Nope. I insisted that if I was to be married to a Duke, then I needed to denounce my former one and take the one that would establish me as his equal. It would be wrong for me to hold a title higher than his. Not to mention the other was only granted to me because my ex-husband sought to make a point." She runs her hands down my shirt and loosens the buttons. "So, I dismissed it and now have a new one that brings a smile to my face."

Since we are disrobing while we talk, I start on her clothes as well. "What is this new title?"

"Duchess Angela Gabriela Perez, Advisor to the King. It's a mouth full, but I believe it is more fitting." Her hand shoves my now unbuttoned shirt over my shoulders. "Have you fucked a duchess before, my Duke?"

I growl and I remove the last of her clothing, admiring her in the black lace covering her breasts and pussy. "No."

"Would you like to?" I wait as she runs her red nails down the center of her body and spreads her legs. Her hand slips under her black knickers and begins doing wicked acts, making her squirm. "I'm getting extremely wet for you."

"Fuck. You are such a tease." I remove my clothes and grab my cock, fist it painfully to keep from coming. "Lick your fingers. Show me how wet you are for me."

She blushes but does as I ask and then rises to her knees. Her lips take the head of my cock and suck on it hard, making me lightheaded. The tip of her tongue toys with the slit until I remove my hand and push it all the way into her fiery mouth. I fuck it slowly while she moans around it, her brown eyes peeking up at me.

I pull free and toss her on the bed, yank her now soaked knickers off of her and spread her wide for me. My cock slides in easily as I hook my elbows under her knees and fall forward. "I'm going to fuck you hard and fast first, make you come on my cock. Then I'm going to slow it down and have you begging me to let you come again. You okay with that?"

Angela slips her bra off and nods. "Yes."

"I love you," I tell her as I slam into her hard and don't stop.

She is whimpering under me, struggling to get the words out, and when she comes, it is magical, and I almost give in to my own release. But I need to slow this down first, so I hold back and do just that.

"Eddie, please," she begs.

"Tell me what I wish to hear."

Angela blinks several times, trying to get her mouth to cooperate with her brain. "I love you too," she finally says.

Those words do it for me, and I spill into her, fall on top of her sweating and panting. I love this woman. Love her like I've loved no one before. It took me long enough to make it here, but now that I am, there will be nothing to stop me from living my best life with her. She is now and will forever be mine, and I'll cherish every day we have together.

Epilogue

ANGELA

I never thought I'd get married again. Not really. My first marriage was a disaster and left a bitter taste in my mouth. So the fact I've been married for a few months now and loving it feels nice.

It's lovely coming home to someone who appreciates me. A man who takes his time to welcome me like only he can. One who goes above and beyond to make sure my days start and end on a positive note.

We are sitting by the fireplace on a pile of blankets, finishing the wine we had with our dinner. He's rubbing my feet while I give him a breakdown of my day. I had to deal with a grumpy bunch of governors who weren't happy about Antonio's recent budget cuts that came down the line last night. It's nice to be able to unload on someone and know he is listening to you. Wants to listen. That he understands getting it off your chest helps you relax and later can get you to relax even more because you've already gotten so much off your mind.

When I'm done sharing, it's his turn. Edward works for the NPB (National Police Bureau) as a Special Investigator. He's trying to figure out who has taken over the Del Markov's territories. This group, if it is even possible, is worse than the one Ruben ran. So, it's my husband's job to find and eliminate them before it gets out of hand. Not his personally, mind you. Edward is the brains of the operation. He has a staff of younger investigators who do the dirty work. His job is to supervise and make sure nothing goes wrong. I may not love his post, but he does, and that is all that matters to me.

Our bottle of wine is about finished and I'm thinking of calling it a night when the front door slams. There aren't a lot of people who just walk into our home. So that limits this person to one of those who can make it past the guards. Not to mention this has been happening more often now that Gabriela has returned. Soon there will be another person entering in a more civilized manner, closing the door with less force.

"Get the fuck out, Gino," Gabriela yells as soon as the door opens. "I'm not your problem, remember. This is my life and I'll live it however I chose to. No one, especially you, gets a say about the choices I make."

He doesn't respond with words. The door closes and then I hear heavy footfalls heading in our direction. The large intimidating male I've gotten to know well these last seven months looms there. His hands are shoved deep in his pockets, a sign he's doing his best to maintain his control. "Did you know about this?"

I realize he's not talking to me. As I direct my attention to my husband, Gabriela comes storming into the room.

"Don't answer him." She steps between Edward and Gino with her arms crossed. "Get out."

He ignores her and asks again. "Did you know what she has been doing up there in Sevilla? What the fuck she's been training for? What she thinks she is going to do as soon as she is properly trained?"

"For your information, I am properly trained already. I passed with flying colors three days ago. I have my assignment and there is not a damn thing you can do about it." I've never seen her this ramped up before. "So fuck off."

They stare at each other for a few moments before she grunts, stomps her foot in that way she's perfected, and twirls to storm off in the opposite direction of him. Her bedroom is down the hall behind us, far away from what she calls the honeymooner's wing.

Gino is dying to go after her, but doesn't, not yet at least. He's not done interrogating Edward, it seems. "Well?"

Edward stands and offers me his hand. "If you are asking me if I knew she entered the academy, then yes."

I blink slowly, confused, wondering why I've not heard about this until now. "What academy?"

"That's not for me to say, love. Gabriela is a grown woman more than capable of making her own choices in life." Edward grabs my hand and kisses it. "We can speak with her in the morning if you'd like. It sounds like she has news she needs to share. I know once you hear her out, you will do what you always have done. You'll support her and trust that she can do anything she sets her mind to."

The proud tone in his voice makes me smile. My daughter is very lucky to have Edward standing by her side. "I look forward to hearing all about it."

"Let's get out of here." He places a palm on my back and leads me toward our suite. "Gino."

"Sir." I can see the war taking place in his eyes.

Edward lays a hand on his shoulder. "The best way to get a woman like Gabriela is to..."

"I don't..." Gino starts to protest, but Edward doesn't permit him to finish.

"Word of advice, son. I've been where you are. I was a coward and thought no one would understand. That I wasn't good enough to love the woman I wanted to be with. I wasted a number of years telling myself that. Don't be like me. Don't allow your ego to get in the way. She's a lot tougher than she looks and has been through her own hell. You might actually be surprised to learn she likely would understand it all more than anyone else would. Stop being the lone wolf who is afraid to let others see him. What do you have to lose by letting that spitfire of a woman see if she can handle the real you?"

I watch Gino shake his head as we walk away to let him digest Edward's words of wisdom. When we are far enough away, I have to ask. "What is going on?"

Edward only smiles down at me before he smacks my arse. "A war. It's going to be a battle of wills. Hopefully, they will both be standing strong when it ends, but that is up to them. No one but those two can fight this war they are about to find themselves in the middle of. We can only watch and pray they don't kill each other first."

HOPE YOU ENJOYED Angela and Edward. Please consider leaving a review on Amazon, Goodreads, and BookBub.

Here is the link to Fearless Warrior, book 5 in The Royals, the story of Gabriela and Gino.

Thank you and happy reading.

The Duke

FALCON GLOBAL NOVELLA

One kiss was all it took...

All I want is my freedom. All my father wants is to chain me to the highest bidder. I have one last opportunity to live on my terms before my choice is taken from me.

Darius Falcon, also known as The Duke, enters my world. He's an arrogant prick who won't take no for an answer. Refusing to change course once he sets his sights on me. Too bad he won't get to keep me for more than a week.

Then one day he materializes from the shadows to save me from a monster. It's then I wonder if now is my chance to take control of over my future. Maybe when you wish upon a hunk, dreams really do come true.

Only Available to Newsletter Subscribers.
https://dl.bookfunnel.com/xn53pw0g4o

Acknowledgments

I'd like to thank my readers. You are who I write for, the people who keep me writing. Thank you, thank you, thank you.

To my beta readers. Thank you to Kimberley for stepping up this time when I needed a first reader. You always make me smile when I read all your thoughts as you read in the comments. I wish I could force all my readers to do that. Thanks to Sally, Abby, and Marie. You ladies always have brilliant suggestions, making my books so much better. Each one of you found issues others missed, assisting me in ways you will never know. I am very grateful to all of you and hope we can work together again in the future.

To Mica Rae, thank you for being you. You are the person I can count on to always have my back. Whenever I need to vent to or just send some silly TikTok, I know you will be there. I'm glad I found you and hope to support you the same way. We got this and together we will be unstoppable.

To Ashley, thank you for helping with all the crazy edits. I hope I am getting better, but believe there will always be those things that I just cannot get right. Your friendship means the world to me. I'm so glad I found you.

To Alyssa for never once complaining when I send her a hundred texts all centered on line edits. She reads them, does her magic, and sends them back. She fixes all the words I just can't seem to get right. And when it is all said and done, she provides the wine and laughs to help me relax and enjoy life. You are my people and I'm so happy we get to hang out and embarrass our girls.

Lastly, I'd like to thank my family. I couldn't do this without their support. I love you all beyond words. None of it would be worth it without the three of you.

*updated 4/20/24

Also by C. R. Riley

Crystal Lake Series

Facing the Storm

Uncharted Waters

Light in the Shadows

When the Fog Lifts

Life Series

The Good Life

A Transformed Life

Love of the Game

Sneaky Quarterback

Tight End Comeback

Scoring the Birdie

Fielder's Choice

Catcher's Interference

Kohl Family Series

Untouchable

Unbreakable

Unforgettable

Unavoidable

Undeniable

The Royals

Suddenly Enthroned

Unexpected Princess

My Noble Fight

Her Royal Highness

Fearless Warrior

About the Author

Contemporary romance author C. R. Riley is celebrated for creating worlds and characters that don't always follow the rules, including those she futilely tries to set herself. But the best characters always find a way around them, often surprising her with their willingness to make each and every journey unique, if not emotionally satisfying.

Her Kohl Family series has been called the perfect epitome of contemporary romance with a twist of the unexpected. The characters tackle tough topics while making you fall in love with them, and despising those baddies who deserve it. Each story is a unique standalone. That cares over in her Modern-Day Royals series, which features characters who are unlike any royal put to the page before. And of course, combining her love of football and baseball she adds a steamy sports romance, Love of the Game which follows a family of athletes on their separate journeys to find true love.

You can find all her romantic and out-of-the-ordinary series on Amazon and free in Kindle Unlimited. Never miss a new project update or book release by signing up for her newsletter or follow her on social media, accounts listed below.

I'd love to hear from you and do my best to personally answer emails.

crriley@crrileyauthor.com

Newsletter Signup:
https://www.subscribepage.com/o5t3m0
Website:
https://www.crrileyauthor.com
LinkTree:
https://linktr.ee/c.r.rileyauthor